ESCAPING POISON
Diaspora Worlds Book Four
Melisse Aires

Copyright

Copyright© Melisse Aires 2014

Table of Contents

Acknowledgements

Editor: G. O'Bryant
This book contains adult subject matter and is intended for readers over age eighteen.
Cover Artist: Melisse Aires
Canstock Photos
Pixabay.com

Newsletter

Please sign up to get emails of new releases and sales.
sendfox.com/melisseaires[1]

---

1. https://sendfox.com/melisseaires

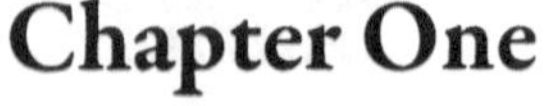

Chapter One

KARVAR SIPPED A GLASS of wine on his terrace overlooking the lights of New Prague Dome. He waited for his bride with a mix of anticipation and satisfaction. The wedding had been perfect, his bride glorious. Tomorrow they would leave for a very long honeymoon. A simple meal had been left for them, since the wedding feast had been sumptuous. They would share the meal and some fine wine before their wedding night.

Brielle was a stunning woman with a fine education, and she moved in the same circles in New Prague Society. They had decided to wait until their wedding night so they could get to know each other better. Introduced to each other by their parents, they had noticed and been amused by the overt matchmaking going on.

The entire wedding and reception had been elegant, thanks to his bride's planning. He'd chosen well. She was lovely, intelligent and well organized, she knew how to ct in every situation. She would never embarrass him.

So what if his brothers thought he was insane.

"You seriously let Mother pick a bride for you?" Kaistril shook his head in disgust. But Kaistril was married to Sabralia, who rescued him as a damaged cyborg from a Gorvas warlord.

It was different for Karvar. He'd stayed here on New Prague the whole time his brothers were having wild adventures with their wives-to-be out in space. He'd been going to work daily, escorting his parents to social events in the evenings, lobbying for certain political causes, officiating ceremonies, helping New Prague's needy. He needed a wife who understood the political climate here, who would promote issues he and his family were trying to change or bolster, who moved comfortably through New Prague High Society... Brielle was perfect.

He heard the door swipe open and turned to greet his bride.

Brielle entered the room. Her dark eyes were huge, and her chocolate brown hair now fell in waves nearly to her waist. Tall and fine-boned, she still managed to have lovely curves under her gown of ivory lace, with gold and pink embroidered and jeweled flowers. Those full pink lips he loved to watch curved into a smile as she walked gracefully toward him. Grace and elegance were her hallmarks.

She toppled over and crashed into the table that held their meal. Food flew everywhere and the crystal carafe of fine wine spilled down Brielle's gown in a blood red splotch before the carafe shattered on the floor. A small cleaning bot rushed out to take care of the mess.

"Brielle," he cried as he rushed to her. She gasped a few times, eyes shut, skin paler than the lace of her gown, and then—nothing. Not even breath.

He hit his arm com. "This is Karvar Anselm, from my suite in the palace. Emergency, medical! Brielle is not breathing." He then started cardiac procedures on his bride.

THEY WOULDN'T LET KARVAR into the medlab. Fury welled up in him. He was a medical doctor, with multiple specialties! He was with her when she collapsed. He got her here to his family's private medical wing still alive. He should be part of this!

The room was soundproof so his sharp rap on the window did nothing. It wasn't a real window anyway, it was a view screen. He wasn't even sure it was in real time. Brielle could be dead right now while he was viewing information ten minutes old.

Karvar flung himself onto the padded seat near the door. There was nothing to do but wait.

What could have happened? She'd been so beautiful at their wedding, smiling and dancing through the reception.

Mother and Kyler, who had just recently taken the position as Protectorate of New Prague as Mother retired, joined him on the bench. He was grateful they sat with him quietly. He had no desire to answer questions right now. Since he had *no* answers.

Sometime later, Father came out dressed in medlab clothes, just long enough to say, "It's drugs. She's an addict."

"Drugs," Karvar repeated, dully. He'd married a drug addict and didn't even know it. Him, an acclaimed research scientist and physician. And a fool, thinking an arranged marriage to a pretty woman from one of the society families would be a shortcut to a real marriage and family. He slumped in his chair, head resting in his hands, elbows on his knees."Will she be all right?"

"I don't know yet, son."

Mother patted his back while Father went back into the medlab. Karvar wondered if Mother thought he was worried because he loved Brielle so. But the truth was he was attracted to Brielle and found her entertaining. He had little real knowledge of her personality or personal decisions. Obviously. Though he knew she loved her little sisters.

Not much to base a marriage on.

How many other times had he sat with his mother, in times of grief and danger? When Kaistril's Tier was attacked and so many New Prague Protectorate Guards just disappeared, no bodies to bury. When Kellac got thrown into prison on an authoritarian tech world. When Kyler disappeared during the Hub Invasion—for months! Karvar had been right here in the dome, living in his suite at the palace, working in his office in the science wing, supporting his parents through the darkest days.

Another hour passed. Mother got up and went to the door of Brielle's room and returned shortly. Father must have messaged her.

"Karvar," His mother spoke softly. "Your father wants us to meet about his findings. He thought it best I be here for it. Kyler, too."

They entered his father's office.

"I'll have a specially trained team inspect your quarters, Karvar." Kyler spoke. "We have also held her maid, housekeeper, hairdresser and other wedding personnel for questioning."

Finally, Father came into the room. He looked pale, with dark circles under his eyes and Karvar was shaken by the contrast of how he had looked at the wedding. Earlier, dressed in the New Prague burgundy and black dress uniform, he had looked healthy, vital. Now the cheerful gleam in his eyes was absent, replaced by shadows. His luxurious, shoulder-length white hair was tucked into a cap. "I'll let you speak to her in a moment, Karvar. She is conscious but weak and needs to rest. Her breathing and speech are not normal."

"It's Ambrosia... but different," he continued. "Far more complex. This is not a simple story of a university child becoming involved in illegal drugs. She was kidnapped and drugged. Groomed, if you will, to marry into a high position here on New Prague. I will have to consult with experts to develop a detox program for her."

Ambrosia was a common intoxicant all throughout the Alliance worlds.

"Where did she get it?" Karvar asked.

"It was supplied for her. Sometimes it was withheld deliberately, to reinforce her handler's power over her. As I said, this is not a typical case of drug addiction." Father paused. "Brielle wants to talk to you."

Karvar nodded and stood to go to her.

Kyler said, "I want your permission to record the talk, in case there are clues we might otherwise overlook."

"Of course."

Karvar entered the room and walked to the bed. Brielle's complexion was nearly the same shade of white as her bedding. Her dark waves were tucked under a stretchy hospital cap and her thick lashes made dark crescents on her skin, a sharp contrast.

"Brielle? You wanted to see me?"

Her eyes fluttered partially open and a tear ran down to the hair at her ear. "I'm sorry, Karvar... couldn't tell you... not fair to you." Her voice was so soft he had to lean over to hear her. "Blackmailed to... spy. Sorry."

More tears fell, sliding to her hair. "Long time... since I went to school. Italy. My sisters threatened... Kyler's children, the older ones... might be targeted. They are ...political. The druggers. Powerful." Her voice came in raspy gasps, though she was on oxygen. "Danger. Please, get them away. My sisters. Don't know who to trust. Don't trust the staff. Don't know who... Don't trust people... Spy could be already be with with them..."

"I can keep them safe."

Her lashes fluttered shut, then opened wider for a moment, luminous light brown and green hazel, so different from most Puregens. "Yes, your family can do it."

She closed her eyes and he wondered if she'd lost consciousness, but she spoke again. "Tell them how I loved them." Tears coursed down her cheeks. "Made it long enough to keep them safe, I hope. Glad for that." Her eyes opened again. "If I die, take my ashes to the sea. Protect my sisters."

Emotion tightened his throat and he couldn't think of anything to say. Brielle was so young, only twenty-three, talking about dying on her wedding night. He nodded and pressed a kiss to her forehead, his mind reeling with painful thoughts and emotions.

He would have helped her if he'd known! She didn't have to keep this a secret. He would have helped. He took a deep breath and concentrated on what to do now.

"I can send them to Farradae with Kellac and Gema. I can get Kellac to leave in the morning instead of next week if your father will let them go."

Her eyes snapped open. "No. Don't tell father... can't trust staff. They were to go to camp on Terra with tutor Mahline..." She drew in breath harshly. "Just take them. Talk to the tutor. Bribe her, invite them over for lunch, anything. Tell Father they were invited to a... an early camp exclusive. Please."

Her eyes shut again, tear sliding down her cheek.

"All right." If her father was involved, it was treason. He was a General in the New Prague Protectorate Guard.

"Thank you." The last was spoken in a whisper of breath.

Karvar rejoined his parents and Kyler in his father's office. Large monitor's of Brielle's room and vitals filled the wall on one side of Father's desk. There were no other medical staffers in attendance.

Father gave a summary of the drug, then said, "Brielle said it was designed so it couldn't be treated at ordinary drug rehab facilities. From what I could see and analyze here, she is correct. I have the lab working on it now. Her kidneys and liver are both shutting down, her heart and lungs are starting to lose effectiveness. I have her on supplemental oxygen, breathing treatments and also a kidney dialysis to take some stress off her body. She is a very sick young woman. Just days, or maybe hours, from death. She is fortunate we could get her to this facility."

"What is her prognosis?" Karvar asked.

Father placed a comforting hand on his shoulder. "I'm am not sure, son. If we can figure out her drug particulars and counteract them, she might do well. Time is a factor." He shook his head. "Luck. If she lives, but has organ damaged, we can eventually clone organs for her, but she will have to be much stronger for a replacement procedure."

"How did this happen so no one noticed?" Kyler asked.

Karvar asked himself the same thing. How could he not have noticed? He was a physician.

But they never had a real courtship, the thought niggled at him. They attended public functions, family dinners. He and Brielle had spent very little time alone together. His research had recently expanded with the acquisition of all the cyborg appliances coming from the cyborg processing plant on Arden, now that travel lanes were safe. He spent long hours in the research lab, and Brielle had never protested.

If we had been a real couple, we would have found time. Private time.

Karvar cleared his throat. "She never appeared intoxicated."

"Brielle will tell us more when she can. It was a long-range plan. They knew she was expected to marry well into New Prague society, and that her father was a military high officer." Father flicked a glance at Karvar and then at Judith. "It succeeded beyond their wildest dreams."

"For the wedding, she had special vials, small amounts in different potencies, to keep her through the day without noticeable drugged behavior. But it was a new procedure and it didn't work as well as her regular drug hits. She began having breathing problems, heartbeat irregularities..."

"Most of her conversation dealt with the danger to her sisters." Karvar said. "Not her father actually. Her sisters. She thinks we need to get her sisters off New Prague. They could go to Farradae with Kellac and Gema. Brielle wants them off-world as soon as possible," Karvar said.

"As soon as we are done here I'll go tell Kellac and Gema. They could leave tomorrow. Kellac and Gema can take them to their station on Farradae or to Farradae City. Either would be safe. My team can quietly extract them and get them on board, get Kellac and Gema on their way," Kyler said.

Karvar said. "We can't trust the tutor."

"Of course. Gema and Kellac have their own crew from Farradae, we will simply let the tutor go with a bonus." Kyler said.

"Good," Karvar said. "But there's something else. Brielle mentioned your grown kids. They could be in danger."

Kyler sat up taller. "They are still at the palace following the wedding. I doubt anyone could have gotten to them there. And I think we were able to contain the emergency to the palace. No one outside of us and two of father's lab staff know she is here."

Mother put a hand on Kylar's arm. "They are young and at home on vacation for a few days. I doubt they are all snuggled in their beds. You wouldn't have been, at that age."

Kyler nodded, his face somber. His three oldest were twenty-two now, Dessa and Tressa were twenty and even little Ambli was nineteen. All of them were old enough to be dancing until the wee hours in the clubs of New Prague.

"We can trace them and contact them by their armcoms?" Mother asked.

"They could all leave with Kellac, though I don't know where he'd put them all. His house isn't that big," Kyler said.

"They could go to Farradae City. Or Kellac could set them up in his hunting tents."

Kyler grinned. "That would be an adventure. I will retrieve them."

Mother and Kyler left to round up the young people and Brielle's sisters.

"Dad, you go get some rest. I'll monitor her and call you if anything changes," Karvar said.

His father nodded. "We are waiting on the lab work."

Father left for the small room in the back of his office that had a bed and Karvar realized he was still wearing his formal wedding suit. He found the staff changing room and changed into plain pull on pants and a baggy shirt with pockets from a medlab closet.

His wedding night, spent in a recliner in his father's private clinic, watching vitals on his new wife.

Towards morning his father woke and took over on the monitors. "Go get some real sleep for a couple hours. The family will all meet at six a.m. in the family living room. From there we'll get the kids to the ship."

"All right."

Karvar went to his suite a few corridors away, thinking how his whole family was now under threat due to his marriage. He sure knew how to pick a bride.

Not that he blamed Brielle.

He entered his suite and halted right inside the door. Something wasn't right. The cushions on his sea-colored couch were not arranged properly. They were supposed to be in a gradient of color, but there, a teal one mixed in with seafoam green. It hadn't been like that when he left. Everything had been perfect for his bride.

Was someone inside?

Slowly he backed out of the room and alerted Kyler on his armcom.

"Hey Kyler, I think someone has been in my rooms."

There was a pause. "In your suite? In the palace? I have not sent a crew there yet."

"Yes."

"Don't go inside. Head straight for the Protectorate Tower. I have a lock on your armcom. Only leave the tower with Kaistril or Kellac. Are you armed?"

"Of course I'm not armed." He was in his home! On his wedding night!

"Kaistril and Kellac will meet you. They are armed."

Thirty minutes later the four brothers inspected his suite. It had been searched, but very subtly. "Probably only someone as particular as you would have noticed," Kyler said.

A member of the royal family had had their suite broken into and searched. Such a security breach had never happened before.

His father messaged him. Brielle had fallen into a coma-like state caused by the drug, they would get no more information from her for the time being.

TYLERIUS GRABBED ANOTHER bottle of mist ale and joined a small group of old school friends on the dance floor. Stars it felt good to not think about studies and asswipe wannabe commanders. On Tailheg there wasn't even a dance bar, just a couple grimy intoxihalls. Excuse him if he was fastidious. He'd been raised on a Hub, dust and dirt were nearly a crime there.

Only three more months, though. Then he'd have a review and head out, a Class Two pilot, headed for the jumpstreams. He shot back the mist ale.

He danced three songs with three different girls, no point on focusing on one when he'd ship out tomorrow evening.

Chip was nowhere to be seen, but then Chip was quite a risk taker where women were concerned. No one had expected tiny Chip Chip Nur to grow in his sixteenth year, nearly a foot, taller than Uncle Kyler. Probably because he looked like a little kid until that summer. By fall all the girls were crazy for him, with his non-Puregen dark skin and muscular build. And then in the years that followed, he packed on muscle like a broadcast gladiator show contestant.

In a Puregen place like New Prague, someone who looked different than the rest of them received lots of attention. Chip Chip had perhaps not handled his new attractiveness as well as he could have.

It was a shock to everyone, especially Grania. They seemed to be getting along fine now, though. It wasn't often that everyone was together, with Chip and the twins in school on Terra and Grania on Mars. While he was stationed at Tailheg, a converted asteroid fuel hub, armpit of the Alliance.

Tylerius craned his neck to see where the fam was. Dessa was dancing with her girlfriend Shay, too slowly to the beat. Ambli... he hadn't seen her all night, wasn't even sure she was at this club. But she'd only been on Terra for a few months of school so all her friends were still here.

She was popular. Ambli definitely wasn't Puregen, being so petite. And she was so pretty, with long dark red hair and gray-green eyes. Round baby face. He grinned and wondered if New Prague parents were now taking pictures of Ambli into the Puregen labs when planning a family. She certainly stood out in a crowd of dark-haired New Prague Puregens.

He was about to call his sort-of-siblings on the family line when his armcom buzzed. A hologram popped up. The secure line. A chill ran through him. It was only used for danger... and he doubted there would be a drill in the middle of Uncle Karvar's wedding night.

His eyechip could read the secure message, while all those around him would see a race flitter commercial.

"This is not a drill. Keep this message open. There has been a breach."

Tylerius jumped on a chair and looked around for the others. Chip charged into the main room from some anteroom, his height making him visible in the crowd. Chip saw him and waved a hand.

Dessa was staring at her screen, holding tight to her girl's hand. Sheesh, what were they going to do with her lover? They couldn't leave her here.

Where the hell was Ambli? And Tressa and Grania? Hopefully they were all together. He messaged on their private kid link. "Where are the girls?" he asked Chip.

"Dunno. They were all dancing together the last I saw."

"I'm joining Dessa and Shay," Tressa's voice came over the com. "Coyt and Loyt are here now."

"Good." Coyt and Loyt were Kyler's personal assistants, extremely competent. "Where's Ambli?" Ty asked when he reached the girls. Grania had joined them, so only Ambli was missing.

Grania looked around. "She ran into friends so she wasn't with us."

"Oh!" Tressa said. "She's wearing a comcuff."

Ty had no idea what Tressa was talking about. "A what?"

Tressa shrugged. "Like a forearm bracelet? You wear it over your armcom, it disables pop-ups."

"Why?" Who would want to disable their com?

"Supposed to symbolize that you are in the moment, not looking for something more interesting to do."

Kids these days. "So she isn't getting the security warning. I'll go look for her. What is she wearing?"

"Short, tight and bright. Turquoise."

"And her hair is down," Grania added.

"While you are looking for her we'll get everyone situated in the transport. I'll come back for you." Coyt and Loyt brothers who were thin, dark and menacing, escorted the others out.

Ty spun around and pushed his way out onto the dance floor again. Where would a really pretty nineteen-year-old girl go?

She might try to flirt with the band, a sorry bunch of toxheads as far as he could tell.

He headed toward the band up front, the crowded dance floor hindering him since he couldn't just shove people out of the way. The lights were dimmed and tuned to the music so different colors flashed over the dancing crowd, making it hard to discern colors.

Short, tight and bright. Her dress had more in common with a swimming suit than a dress. Star Gods, she had great legs, long, smooth muscle, delicate knees and ankles. Towering high heels, which she could actually move in. She was on a small raised platform with a handful of others. A couple of faces looked familiar. Academy kids from Ambli's year.

He leaped up on the platform.

"Ty," Ambli cried and threw her arms around him, just as the band segued into a slow song. All the lights dimmed even more.

"Ambli, your arm cuff," He started to explain, but Ambli, wiggled against him. His reaction was completely sexual. He wasn't going there, even though he'd had that interest in her for a long time. She wasn't really his sister after all, and they had spent most of their childhoods separated by his Academy schooling. He grabbed her upper arms and eased her away from him. "Come on Ambli. We need to go. There's a security alert, some kind of trouble."

"Trouble? What are you talking about?"

"I don't know what happened, but Coyt and Loyt are here to take us back to the palace."

Coyt met them and with Ambli between them, they hustled out of the club to a waiting transport. It flew to the Protectorate Palace transport pad and they all rushed into the family room in Grandmother's quarters. All the uncles were in attendance. Ty felt a chill run down his spine. Had something happened to Grandma? Were they under attack? But then his grandmother joined them.

She sat down in an overstuffed chair, looking tired. "I'll get right to it. Karvar's wife Brielle was blackmailed to be a high-level spy. The blackmail came in the form of a specially tailored drug, which she has been on for a number of years. But her health was perhaps more fragile than her handler's knew. She was given special doses to take through these busy wedding days, and she collapsed tonight. She will probably live, but we are not completely sure yet.

"Before she went into a coma, she was awake for a few minutes. She said her sisters and all of you are under threat."

Kyler took a deep breath. "We are taking this seriously. The drug she was addicted to is a specialized compound, not some street drug anyone could buy. Karvar's personal suite was searched... you know how detailed he is... someone didn't put something back in the right order. Or else we wouldn't have known."

"I'm taking my family and Brielle's young sister's to Farradae in two hours. We don't think the handlers know Brielle is in Dad's medlab," Kellac said. "We want them to think they are having their honeymoon as planned. But we'd like to send you all to Farradae. I can use diplomatic channels to cover for your absence at school and at the Tailheg training facility, Ty."

Chip gasped and flopped back on the couch. "I can't go anywhere. My dissertation outline is due in sixty days! I need to be connected to the Alliance Orion Library. Can't reach that on Farradae!"

Kyler looked at Kellac, eyebrows raised.

"No way to connect from Farradae," Kellac said.

Kyler frowned. "I don't want to split them up. We don't have enough guards I feel confident about."

Kaistril spoke. "The diplomatic compound on Chen Chen would be safe."

Kyler nodded his head. "But public. No way you can hide five family members there."

"I have the same problem," Grania said. "Everyone in our year has to get their outline done in sixty days."

"Couldn't we stay here?" Chip said. "Anywhere I have a connection to the library. And a quiet space to work." Grania nodded.

After some discussion they decided to send them all, Shay included, and Ty, down to the Recondin Science Station in a remote region of the southern continent, called the Big Poison.

Chapter Two

BIG POISON SCIENCE Dome, Decommissioned
New Prague Southern Continent.

Brielle heard her husband's light footsteps as he came up the spiral stair to the loft. She pried her eyes open and looked at the bedside medcom. Not time for another treatment... her heart thudded. Perhaps bad news... Trouble. Or maybe the treatment wasn't working.

Karvar strode into the room wearing a white lab coat over thin knits. Golden streaked brown hair moved as he walked since he wore it rather long and it waved around his neck. Golden eyes, framed in protective glasses, turned on her. Brielle sat up straighter and smoothed her hair.

"I heard from Kellac. They all arrived safely on Farradae, and Gema and the children are already in a forest village some miles inland from Farradae City. None of the villagers have any ties to New Prague, or really any way to communicate. It is just too remote."

"They are safe." The relief brought tears to her eyes.

"Yes, they are well hidden. Gema says they will join the other village children for school and activities."

"I hope they have fun. I hope they aren't scared."

Karvar paused. Normally he left her as soon as possible, but he knew she genuinely cared for her sisters.

"Gema and Kellac will be good to them. Gema is a warm person. And the Farradae community is friendly. I think they will have a fine visit there."

"It is warm there—like here? A rainforest?"

"It is tropical and they are near the sea. The girls are with Gema in an inland village. There is a high cliff riddled with shallow caves, and that is where the Farradae lived at first. When the Gorvas attacked a few years ago, the Farradae fled from the city to the caves and there was not one life lost."

"I'm glad they will be safe."

"The jumpstream to Farradae is only known to a few, and traveled by even fewer. They are safe. Gema said there is a pool with a waterfall for swimming. It sounds lovely. And it is Terraformed. Not like this jungle."

"I see."

"Well," he said. "You should get some rest."

"Yes. Thank you for coming to tell me. It is a weight off my mind." She paused. "I wonder how my father is taking the separation."

"He thinks they took an early transport to their camp on Terra. We falsified an early camp offer, some kind of cultural opportunity. No one can locate them. Not even him."

Karvar walked toward the door to leave. "Tomorrow I will set up the float chair. You only need drips twice a day now. And if you get tired the chair reclines. You'll be able to come downstairs."

"Can I go out into the fenced area?" A tall fence surrounded the science station, filled with transplanted flora the scientists collected over the years.

He nodded. "With a breather mask you can. The pollen counts are a little high and your immune system is weak right now. We don't want to chance Pollen Plague."

She shuddered. "Definitely not."

THE NEXT DAY AFTER her morning medications, Karvar put her chair together. It was not large, but it was comfortable and even had a small table and cup holder she could position over her lap. Which she probably would. Karvar went over the instructions to make sure she would be safe in it. She could actually float down to the lower level which housed the kitchen and living room. Karvar had put her bed and medical equipment in the loft where there was more room.

She was so tired of being ill.

Technically, for the first time in years, Brielle was free from the drug. Now she just needed to recover from the long-term effects, especially on her heart and lungs. It wouldn't be long and she would actually be well, at least as well as she was going to be after years of the drug. She would need a procedure to replace her heart and lungs with healthy cloned organs sometime in the future.

She hadn't thought that day she was drug-free would ever be in her reach. Brielle couldn't help feeling grateful to Karvar. He could have annulled the marriage, sent her back to her life. She would have continued to spy and maybe ended up in prison where her withdrawal wouldn't have been handled by the best medical facility in the Terran Alliance. She would have died. She had so much to be thankful for.

But she was impatient. She wanted to move, she wanted to go outside the dome and look at the plants, the flowers...

They were to stay here for two months, maybe longer. Karvar's brother Kyler was investigating her contacts, looking for who was drugging her. Until they were found, she and Karvar would live in hiding.

Carefully Brielle floated down the stairs, making sure to go slowly enough so she wouldn't get dizzy. Karvar had a workstation set up by a window, cyborg parts were strewn all over it.

She watched him work for a while, not wanting to disturb him. She floated over to an observation window and looked through to the fenced forest area around the station. Maybe later, when she wasn't so tired, she would chat with him again. She fell asleep in the warm sunshine.

BRIELLE LOOKED BETTER, Karvar noticed. More color in her face. SHe could speak sentences without running out of breath now. She'd lost quite a bit of weight since the treatment began two days after their wedding. It would be a while before she quit looking so fragile. If she ever did. Her heart and lungs were compromised.

He wondered if Kyler had identified her handlers yet. It was a few days before the satellite would be in a position to communicate with him. Karvar jotted his question on his armcom so he wouldn't forget.

He missed his colleagues, both here in New Prague and at the new cyborg recovery camp on Arden. They messaged frequently with their findings, brainstorming issues as they unraveled the cyborg appliances. This tech, taken from Arden, the hidden planet his brother Kyler had found, wasn't Gorvas. Some had applications that went back to early Terran prosthesis works, but the other stuff... a real leap in technology. Perhaps alien? A high tech Zh Cle' colony somewhere? Or the people, the Recondin. They certainly had unusual tech, but no one had seen metallic appliances to enhance bodily functions among the Recondin. They had advanced healing, but it was organic. Karvar's background was medical engineering, working with the machines that medlabs used rather than with sick people. Though he was more than capable of handling Brielle's detox since the correct drug compounds were made for her.

Detox. His bride. What a mess. Hopefully, her handlers that forced the drug on her would be caught soon. Considering that few labs could make such a high-level intoxicant, keyed to Brielle's body chemistry, narrowed down their search quite a bit. Kyler was working with the Terran Premier since the initial incident took place there.

"Can I go outside in the chair?"

He pushed up his focals. She wanted to go outside? Seemed an odd desire for a society girl. "Are you sure? There is a perimeter fence, but flying things can get in."

"During the day most of the predators are sleeping, aren't they?"

"Oh sure. It is safe enough to go out inside the fence. You'll have to wear a breather though."

"Of course."

He got two breathers and helped her put hers on, then opened the lock that kept the unfiltered air out. They went out into the humid yard.

"I can still smell the flowers."

"Yes, the breathers only keep out the spores that are fairly large."

"Is there data in the station database that I could access? I'd like to see the research on the local flora."

She rolled her chair right into a thick stand of flowering vines, which made him a little nervous. What if there were biting things in there? He followed her. She was cupping a bloom, gently feeling the fuzzy yellow petals.

"I'm sure there is. While you are resting after lunch I'll pull it up."

"I'm sure I'll be fine out here. I'll stay right near the windows," Brielle said, still looking at the plants.

"Right. I'll check on you in a little while." Karvar set a timer for every fifteen minutes.

TEN DAYS LATER:

Brielle was thrilled she was getting stronger. She could now walk across her room to the hygenie without getting out of breath, and she was down to one nap a day, not three. The pain that washed her body, cramping her stomach, making her head and heart pound when she was overdue for the drug, was gone. And with that, the anxiety she'd lived with so long lightened. She tired easily, but woke refreshed. The float chair was still needed to get around, her weak legs could buckle if she did too much, but she could look forward to the day when she would have normal movement. A normal life.

She joined Karvar in the mornings, fixing her preferred blended greens and protein drink, which she happily made all by herself. She sat in her float chair and drank the liquified greens while he ate a more normal breakfast of bread and fruit.

"You are working on focals." His table by the window had crates stacked next to it and parts were everywhere.

"Yes. My eyes have a genetic defect, for which I had an implant, but I find the different cyborg focal appliances fascinating. And if my eyes should fail again, I might be able to incorporate some of the technology. Some of it is so different than what we are producing in the Alliance medical industry. It is like a revelation."

He had never spoken so long or with such enthusiasm since they had arrived at the Big Poison Station. He grinned, looking a little sheepish. "Since my sight has not always been good, I enjoy trying different focal appliances. Having a great deal of different visual data to explore is exciting. I figured I would need something to do while you recovered."

"How old were you when you got the implants?"

"Twelve. Had it done on Terra. Afterward, we went on a family camping trip in the Rocky Mountains."

She smiled. "Lovely there! I went on a school trip to the Rockies when I was in boarding school. I find the outdoors fascinating and want to spend time exploring. It is wonderful to have an interest to follow, and the means to do it."

They soon fell into a routine where Brielle exercised in the small pool on the lower level after breakfast while Karvar used the other equipment while keeping an eye on her in the pool. After that, she dressed and went outside to listen to the trillers and see what had bloomed while she slept. They lunched together and she napped, while having an IV treatment. In the afternoon, since Karvar was busy with the crate of cyborg eye parts, she spent time studying the plant data he downloaded from the station com, often out in the shade near a stand of flowers. Her new armcom—since Kyler had kept her old one for his investigation —was nearly empty of data. She was thrilled to find she could have the entire station archive with her, an amazing body of work, going back more than three hundred years, when Terrans first settled the planet.

The float chair took her deeper into the wild growth, but she was able to stand and walk around an area for some time now, examining greenery more closely. She loved the dense darkness of the jungle. She took a blanket to the pool and sat there in the warm shade, watching the trillers flit from flower to flower. They were so cute, like fuzzy pastel bats with delicate wings, listing from flower to flower, pinks, lavenders, greens and yellows, and rarer turquoise ones. She never saw them in bright light, not even where there were many flowers; they preferred shade and were thickest in dark undergrowth. They had long tongues like a butterfly's to reach nectar inside flowers. The fuzzy, puffy body hair collected pollen. The trillers lived in small flocks and would spend time each day grooming each other. The pollen they licked off each other was another important part of their diet, according to the report she read.

One afternoon she found a triller flock whistling and fluttering in one area, clumped together. She slid off her chair and moved slowly toward them to investigate. One tiny triller was on the ground trying to loft, but one delicate, fuzzy wing was limp.

"Oh." Brielle didn't think it could bite so she cupped it in her hands. It was as long as her smallest finger, a puff of lilac fluff with patterned fuzz on her wings, darker lavender swirls with specks of green. It cried a piteous whistle, the tiny soft body quivering. Large, round dark eyes and small circle mouth gave it an eerily human face, with a frill of vertical feathers like a tiny crown.

Karvar might know if the wing needed set. She got back in her float chair and flew back to the dome as fast as she could. Brielle gently smoothed its fur. "I'll take you home. I will gather flowers so you can feed. You can live there in safety until your wing recovers."

"Karvar, Karvar!" She called for him while she waited for the lock to push out the unfiltered air and the inner door to open.

When the door light turned green Karvar burst into the lock. "What's wrong, what happened?"

His golden eyes roved all over her, looking for wounds, but his gaze made her feel hot. Weak at the knees.

She really was getting better. *This is attraction. Desire.* She had always considered him to be a handsome man. Brielle yanked off the ugly breather.

"I found a hurt triller." Her voice came out breathy.

He reared back. "Oh. I thought maybe you got hurt."

"No. I feel fine. But can you help the triller? I think her wing might need help."

He moved back to his worktable and she got out of her chair.

She frowned. "Trillers don't like bright light. Can you close the sun shade and dim your lights?"

"Sure." He quickly pulled on a cyborg visor and lowered the lights. He handled the tiny creature gently and soon had a simple splint tied on with gauze.

The tiny triller seemed to know it was to help her. The blue shade of its snout shade indicated a female.

"It probably feels better to be wrapped. We'll undo it in a few days to see how it is healing," Karvar said.

"She can live in the indoor plants up in the loft, and I'll make sure to bring cut flowers in for her to feed."

Brielle floated up the stairs in the chair—stairs were still exhausting—and set the triller under a flowering plant. Then she had to get her a tiny dish of water. The little flyer sipped from the water and then maneuvered herself deep into the center of the plant.

"A nap sounds like a good idea."

HOW HAD SHE STAYED so beautiful? Karvar often found himself watching Brielle as she moved about the station. He couldn't figure it out. The drug she was addicted to was a poison, and she'd been on it since her teens. But nothing betrayed any form of illness. Perfect, creamy skin, supple flesh. She had gained a little weight since the treatment started. Her long legs were lightly muscled, her breasts, while not overly large, were round... enticing. She had a lovely shape and now that she was recovering, he could tell she had a feminine yet athletic build.

Big dark eyes, and that hair. Thick waves of shiny, chocolate brown, falling to her waist. The little triller she'd rescued clung to the hair near her ear, peeping out like an exotic lilac flower.

"How did you stay healthy?"

Brielle swung around from the fruit plate she was making, an expression of surprise on her face.

"You never showed any signs of illness, yet my father said you were just weeks, maybe days, from organ failure."

She walked to his table, carrying a cup of tea and a variety of fruits and vegetables on a small tray. Her hips swayed in an unconscious sensual rhythm and Karvar felt sweat break out. *That's why you didn't annul the marriage. Had nothing to do with diplomacy or political fallout. Those legs...*

"I have a secondary degree in botany."

That surprised him. "Oh. I thought you graduated with a degree in Alliance Law."

"I did. Really, I had few choices. Terran Alliance law, or Alliance contract law. At least the Constitutional studies held an overview of Diaspora history. That was the most interesting part of the degree." She sat down a nibbled on sliced fruit.

"After I attempted to detox when I was sixteen—it was a failure, I was back on the drug in a week— I went to a few doctors, who couldn't help me. Then I went to an herbalist. I saw the ad in an old-fashioned paper circular, hung on a post. Quaint. But one day I went down to the barrio and found the herbal shop. It was owned by an elderly couple from Ecuador, a place that has protected old growth forests. Amazing such a thing still exists on Terra. Anyway, I paid for a private consultation. It took all day. They drew blood and everything.

"Mana, the old woman, developed a diet and herbal remedies to keep me as strong as possible. Eventually, I learned how to grow some of the plants myself... a nice little hobby, growing tropical plants. And my handlers ignored it."

They were silent for a while as Karvar tried to picture a teenaged Brielle growing plants and making herbal remedies.

And I was lucky to have a natural babyface, as they call it. It kept me from looking exhausted and haggard."

"Someday, if this really works, I want to contact Mana and Silas. Let them know I got help. Give them a gift..."

"So, herbal treatments helped keep me healthy. The plant world had answers to my body's needs. And I did a type of slow movement exercise to keep my muscles toned. I didn't add to the abuse with alcohol or other things like that."

She hit her armcom and pulled up a holo. "My new com, the one Kyler replaced my old one with... it now holds all the plant and weather data this station ever collected. Fabulous."

Brielle scrolled through data as she ate veggie chips and a protein dip. "Near that pool, on the far southeast corner of the compound, there is a Neon Orchid. They bloom on two moon nights, which is tomorrow night. I really want to see it. Can we take a trip there tomorrow night?"

Two moons, a pool, a flowering rare flower, his stunning bride. Karvar cleared his throat. "We will have to wear breathers. Pollen's always worse at night."

Thank the star gods, or he'd do something stupid. She only married him to survive, after all. "Sure. I'll check out that large flitter. It will hold two people. I expect it is in good working order, but I'll double check."

She smiled, showing those dimples and white teeth. "Wonderful."

THE FLITTER WAS A TRIANGULAR shape, large enough to carry four passengers. It had a hold for supplies and equipment and some type of emergency equipment was bundled inside. Karvar added a fresh water container and some snacks. He was a little surprised at his enthusiasm for the short trip. Really, since arriving at the Big Poison Station he'd taken care of Brielle's medical needs and worked on the ocular devices he'd brought with him, while he ignored this whole exotic world.

He'd traveled down to Recondin fields when they were brand new, with Kyler and the first team of scientists assembled, but they had not ventured north to the rainforest. All his life he heard how dangerous the Big Poison continent was, so other than the trip to the Recondin Fields he's spent no time here. Few New Prague citizens had ever been here. New Prague's emphasis was on spaceship building and military manufacturing concerns so the natural beauty of the southern continent was largely ignored. The planet's population was largely transient, workers stayed on the planet just long enough to fulfill a contract with a factory.

Now all the science stations in the rainforest were closed. The Recondin field station was in the far south where great temperate grasslands existed, where the living ship had deposited her seeds. That station was thriving.

Several years ago, at the beginning of the Gorvas invasion, all three of Karvar's older brothers had disappeared and later turned up with wives. Kaistril had been gone the longest. He'd been turned into a cyborg servant belonging to Sabralia, who he later married. Then Kellac had been imprisoned on trumped up charges on a distant Alliance world, and while he awaited diplomatic solutions he'd participated in a view-cast wilderness survival game. He'd returned with his wife, Gema. Just as Kaistril had been found, Karvar's oldest brother, Kyler, assisting Gema's and Kellac's to escape from Gorvas Hunters. Kyler got separated from the New Prague rescue force and ended up on a ship full of orphans, escaping the Gorvas takeover of the space hub.

Kyler had shown up a year later or so in a strange bioship, a type of spacefaring plant called a Recondin, with wife Skyleen and a large adopted family, plus a new baby on the way. The interior of the Recondin was formed into oceans and continents, with a livable atmosphere, by a race of humanoid people. Later it was determined by scientists that the Zh Cle', the Terrans, and the people of the Recondin all shared distant common ancestry. Kyler and the orphans had lived there quite well until the ship arrived in orbit near New Prague. The Recondin had seeded the southern lowlands of the continent and the plants were already thriving. Some goruds were getting enormous.

For all those years of excitement and danger for his brothers, and the years since then when they had been happily growing their families, Karvar had remained on New Prague, working in the research lab. He'd watched his older brothers and their marriages and families, but nothing exciting like that had happened in his life, even though he wanted to marry and have a family.

Then about a year ago, as his mother adjusted to life as the former Protectorate of New Prague since Kyler had taken over the position, she had confided something to him.

"I love all my daughters-in-law. Each is unique and strong, and my sons are happy. But I am old fashioned it seems. I still wish one of my sons had married into one of the New Prague families that have stood by us so loyally all these years. That is how I met your father, after all, and I have such fond memories of that time, the dances, the dinners..."

It was then that Karvar decided to marry one of the society daughters he met continually at social events with his parents, a wife from a powerful family of New Prague.

He went back into the dome and ran up the metal stairs to the loft where Brielle was resting. She rolled over on her bed as he entered the room and her lips curved in a smile. His heart revved. Bare arms, a sleep gown in white, plain serviceable clothes, but on her the white knit seemed to bring a glow to her skin. He'd seen her nude, of course, caring for her in the early days, and the knowledge that she had small, dark brown nipples contrasting with her creamy skin suddenly froze his brain. She was far too beautiful to be relaxed around.

Karvar barely managed to gather his thoughts. "The flitter is in good shape. I packed in some snacks though it has some survival packs in the storage area that are still good. We'll be wearing breathers, but the cab of the flitter has filtered air so we only need them outdoors."

He had to concentrate on the news he brought. *Maybe this marriage isn't dead in the water.*

He stopped that thought. Of course, his marriage was dead. It had been under false pretenses, and who knew how Brielle would handle life now she was no longer drugged? It was over.

"Perfect."

BRIELLE SQUIRMED IN her seat with excitement. She had read about this rare flower years ago and always dreamed of seeing it bloom. And she was here with Karvar, who looked so handsome in the two moons' light. His hair was a little longer than at their wedding, curling around his neck, and he wore plain, dark green coveralls, the kind the station had in the laundry. She wore similar coveralls, but hers were a silvery gray, made of a thin, stretchy fabric, very comfortable. Inside the flitter they did not need the breathers, and he was wearing a thin pair of focals that left most of his face bare, like old-fashioned eyeglasses.

She secretly approved and thought the focals actually emphasized his gorgeous golden eyes and fine cheekbones. Her husband was handsome but so unconscious of it. He wasn't a flirt or ladies' man, though he could have had his pick as he'd wandered through the salons and dinner parties of New Prague society. He'd been totally unconscious of the competitive games society daughters played for his attention.

The pool was at the bottom of a rock outcrop, with a small waterfall. Previous crews had removed some large plants and covered the ground with gravel so there was a landing area and a small beach. Since it was inside the perimeter, large predators were kept out, though there were other jungle denizens that could prove troublesome. Karvar had a laser gun and Brielle carried a personal zapper.

Flocks of pastel trillers, like drifts of floating blossoms, showed clearly in the bright two moonlight as they moved through the vegetation, hunting for food, and Brielle had brought Lila, her rescued triller, along. She thought it might be a good place to release her back into the wild.

Night blooming flowers were everywhere, some large, others tiny, growing in clusters of blue or gold. The pool reflected the tiny glowing blossoms and the two moons above, the larger one silvery, the smaller streaked aqua and blue. A stand of reeds along the shoreline glowed pale green. Brielle set up the graphic recorder on her armcom, she wanted to capture all of this. "This is stunning."

Karvar grinned and handed her a breather. "Really is, I'm glad you talked me into coming." She pulled on her breather and slid out of the flitter. Karvar followed her.

"There, it is starting to open."

The plant was tall with long, waxy leaves, and rose a few feet over their heads. The blossom was twisted closed, but as they watched, it slowly unfurled. It was a neon purple bloom, glowing in the jungle undergrowth.

Brielle used her com to take pictures. "That is the most gorgeous thing I've ever seen." Even through the mask her voice was breathy with excitement. Karvar grinned at her enthusiasm.

THEY STAYED FOR SOME time. Brielle took pictures of the pool and other glowing flowers, and of the drifts of trillers moving from the plant to plant. Her own small triller, now named Lila, flew awkwardly to the plants and flocks, but constantly returned to Brielle, perching on her head like an exotic flower.

"I really thought she would leave and join the other trillers," Brielle said later as they moved toward the flitter to leave. "She flies well enough now to feed herself."

A thundering roar filled the air and bright, sharp light burned through the forest. Brielle screamed and Karvar pulled her down behind a tree. Debris flew through the forest, plants and bark ripped up and thrown by the force of engine backdrafts.

He dragged her to the flitter and gunned it into a vertical climb. As they breached the canopy there was a wall of fire in the direction where their dome had been. Far above it glided a New Prague starfighter, its triangular shape and light pattern familiar to Karvar.

"Make sure you are harnessed. I'm diving." Before they vanished into the greenery he took some frames of the ship with his focal. There might be a designation they could use to find who flew the ship.

"We need to hide." He plowed the small ship into a thick stand of vines and bushes, coming to stop. He pulled Brielle out of the ship. They still wore their breathers.

"There are no large animals within the fence that could hide our body heat signatures. Our bodies will be the only thing of human mass around." He began grabbing vegetation. "We have to hide the flitter."

She joined him, ripping large round leaves and ferns from the soil. Soon the flitter was completely covered.

"Come on." Karvar grabbed her hand and dragged her through the forest to the pool. "The water will disguise our body heat. I'm sure three are no large predators. The station keepers eliminated as many threats as they could."

Karvar hopped in. The water was only to his chest. He held out his arms and she screwed her eyes shut and jumped.

The water was cool, not slimy or anything. There were plants on the bottom brushing against her legs, which she could feel through her thin leggings. He held her close, which was far too comforting, but odd, because they only touched when necessary.

"Reeds." Karvar moved them to the far shore, which had a growth of reeds reaching a couple feet above the water level. They moved into the middle of them.

A bright light zoomed overhead

"Quiet now." Karvar breathed right into her ear.

Lila, her triller, found them and fluttered wildly, along with a handful of her friends. Brielle started to wave them away.

"No." Karvar caught her hands and pulled them down. "Looks natural. Wildlife..." Karvar whispered and she held still. The air of the night was warm, but she was already feeling cold in the water. The bright light moved on but then came back overhead. Brielle began to shiver. Karvar wrapped his arms around her and held her pressed tight to his front for warmth. A drone, not large, but menacing, with lights and ocular devices on swiveling appendages, swept through the clearing. Lila and the trillers went crazy, whistling warnings and fluttering wildly.

It left. They waited, silent, but both breathing hard. Brielle couldn't control her shivering.

"Maybe they are gone."

They waited quite a while, straining to hear the hum of machinery through the whistles of the trillers. Karvar lifted her to the side of the pool and her teeth chattered uncontrollably. He wrapped his arms around her and rubbed her back trying to provide some heat through friction. The trillers settled back to flying between flowers. Lila, flitting around a flower cluster suddenly beelined back to Brielle, followed by a handful of other trillers.

"It's coming back," she whispered. Karvar nodded and they jumped back into the shallow water of the reeds.

Two drones entered the clearing and it might have been her imagination, but they seemed more aggressive than the one before. They traversed the clearing in a grid pattern, even moving across the pool. "Under!" Karvar whispered in her ear.

Brielle gulped a deep breath and Karvar pulled her under. A drone got closer, parting the fronds. Would it see them? Or capture a picture humans readers would recognize as people in the water? Panic and lack of breath filled her, she wanted to move. Karvar clamped his arms around her tight, holding her still under the water. She forced herself to be still but she wanted to fight him, to flail to the surface.

It was getting closer. She was going to drown. Her body screamed for air!

Lila and her triller flock flew to the drone, landing and fluttering around it as if it was a nectar filled bloom. More trillers came to join until the drone was surrounded by a cloud of trillers. The drone raised and lowered, dodged right and left, but the cloud of trillers persisted, landing on its lights and mechanical eyes.

"Fast!" Karvar urged her up for a quick breath, and then they were back under the water.

The drones finally zipped away and they surfaced, drawing in deep gulps of air but just above the water, still hidden in the reeds.

"I think it is gone, but we need to stay here."

"My breather came off when we jumped in."

Karvar pulled his breather over her face. "They didn't find the flitter that I could tell. They didn't push into those vines. Let's get you in there, there are dry clothes you can in a cupboard in the back. I'll go back and look for the breather."

She was terrified, but wasn't sure she could manage more cold water. Teeth chattering, she let Karvar half carry her to the flitter. He found her a towel and then put their only breather on and slipped back out to the pool to find the lost breather. She pulled off her wet clothes and dressed in a soft green coverall like Karvar wore. Then she watched anxiously from the back window where a small break in the foliage showed the pool in the light of the Neon Orchid.

The drones did not return. Karvar had to re-enter the pond to find the breather floating in the reeds. Then he joined her in the flitter.

"I think we're safe here. Safe enough. We'll stay here until near dawn, and watch for the ship or more drones to come back."

"There's fire." She pointed through the flitter window. "That's where the station is. Was."

"Yes. It was stupid of me to take the flitter up like that. I don't know what I was thinking. A flitter like this has no real speed. They must have seen a bit of movement."

"It looks like someone tried to kill us, Karvar. Me, probably, more than you. And it is difficult for anyone to think straight when they are in such a situation. You kept us alive."

"I confess I have not been in such situations, unlike my brothers, since I never joined the military or saw combat. But I think we should hide here for a while, figure out what to do in the morning."

Karvar clambered to the back to the storage hold. "Here's a heat-keeper blanket."

After he dried off they ate a snack. Brielle was grateful for the blanket, after a while she started to warm up. He wasn't cold at all, it seemed. "Must be something to do with my treatment, that I am so cold."

"Yes, you are not yet at one hundred percent."

Brielle was not able to take her meds but that seemed trivial with a ship firing on them. She could not stay awake, though she wanted to take her turn at watch.

"Sleep, Brielle. I can keep watch tonight. This is far more activity than you should be having at this point in your recovery."

"All right." She still felt guilty, but if she didn't rest she might be even more exhausted tomorrow.

Brielle woke to a near-night grayness. Dawn was coming, she could hear trillers and other rainforest callers waking. "Did you get any sleep?"

"A couple hours. I stayed awake until around two, but then decided they weren't coming back." Karvar handed her a protein snack and a jug of water.

"So what do we do now?'

"Not sure. We can't communicate until the satellite comes back around in three days. The storage hold has a canopy camp, the type we drop down onto the treetops, then we can land the flitter in the center. But we don't have solar powered breathers. Ours will be out of power in a couple hours."

"There is no way to charge them? And the flitter? It will be out of power soon, too?"

"The flitter has a solar collector. We can hook it up several hours each day."

"So we just need to sit tight until we can contact Kyler."

Karvar nodded. "I'm uncomfortable staying here, though. I'm afraid they might check back here in a day or two, just to make sure they got us. I was thinking of landing in the undergrowth near the dome and going to see what might be salvageable. Then we go camp somewhere until we can reach Kyler."

"All right." She hoped there was something to salvage.

Karvar flew through the undergrowth but landed in a vine-covered nook between trees.

"Stay here. If I see anything move I'll hide and attempt to get back to the flitter."

He grabbed their one weapon, slipped out and crept to the smoking ruins. Brielle waited, tense, hoping there was no danger there.

He came back carrying a container, which he put down near the back of the flitter.

"A whole area of the lower dome survived. I think a water system doused flames. We lucked out. I'm going to bring a couple more boxes."

He carried back more containers and a few boxes. Brielle got out and helped him stow the gear in the back. "Food. More protein bars, some tea and other drinks. Some of your meds were stored there, which will help you. Also the cyborg appliances I hadn't looked at yet. Grabbed a couple large cooking pots. We might have to boil drinking water."

"Or collect rainwater."

"Right."

"I HAVE THE BIG POISON Station data downloaded onto my armcom. We can pull up maps," Brielle said.

They'd flown away vaguely south of the dome, but really had no plan.

Karvar agreed and hovered the ship while Brielle pulled up a holoscreen map.

"This is the first research station, White Plume. It is still standing, but it doesn't have a dome and has no perimeter fence still standing. But a group of scientists camped there six years ago." She indicated the place, up in the center of the rainforest, west of them.

"There's the mountains." She pointed some distance south. "The Recondin fields are in the plains on the south side of the mountains... several stations there."

"It would take a long time to get there in the flitter," Karvar said. "The Big Poison is four times larger than New Prague continent, so we are looking at days of travel. I'm not sure any of the mountain passes are safe for this flitter, either. I don't think I would like to try to push it up in high altitudes."

She nodded. "And the Recondin field stations are well known. The news was full of articles on the Recondins a few years ago. Our attackers might look for us there."

"I think those stations are safe. That's where some of Kyler's grown kids are staying until they are cleared to go back to University. His younger ones were placed in summer camps on Chen Chen. I know they have token security forces with them since there's the occasional crazy who wants to turn one of the Recondins into his very own spaceship."

"So if we could get down there we would be able to communicate normally."

Karvar nodded.

Brielle pointed northwest of their current location. "This old station, Glim Falls. I think it is buried in the Station data. It was last used more than a century ago, but crews traveled there to see the falls. Doesn't say if they stayed inside or just did day trips."

"Let's head there. Maybe there are supplies. Old breathers."

Not having breathers they could recharge was a problem. So far pollen counts hadn't been too high, but that could change.

"What do you think will happen since I can't take all the meds?"

Karvar shifted in his seat. "I'm not sure. You are cleared of the drug, so you won't have withdrawals. The medication I was able to retrieve was the most important, immune support to keep you from catching other illnesses while you are still weak. I think you will experience fatigue, mainly. And you will be vulnerable to infections and illness."

"Lung fever due to the spores."

"Yes. You will be more vulnerable to Pollen Plague. But we will be in touch with Kyler in three days. Even without breathers, we should be fine. We'll be able to get treatment before we have compromised breathing."

KARVAR FLEW UNTIL LATE afternoon. "I don't want to be setting up the base on the canopy in low light. Just in case." They'd been traveling north for some time but would not reach the old station for some hours.

"I think that's wise. We wouldn't want to slide and land on the ground."

"Luckily the flitter has a soft landing autopilot."

"That's good. But you know about the mud, right?"

"What about the mud?" Karvar glanced at her, a slight frown marring his forehead.

"Well, it wasn't an issue inside the fence, but out in the jungle you don't want to get too close to the mud. Some of it is really deep, more like a pond. There are animals called mud salps. Kind of like a big slug, except they are predators. And territorial. They swoop up from the mud and grab birds as they fly by, or animals that venture too close."

"Surely they wouldn't try to eat something this size."

"No. But there are records of ships being damaged. Some of the salps get huge and can stretch upwards to sixteen feet. And they could eat a human. Or at least a leg or something. Or drag you into the mud and drown you."

"Star god's balls." Karvar pulled up a dozen feet. "Help me by finding the canopy camp instructions, all right?" He should have prepared better for an outing. What the hell was he thinking? He barely knew how to use the damn equipment.

Brielle found the information and read it out loud.

"Ready? I'm going to launch the base and land the flitter."

The base was a type of large mesh floor that rested on the treetops. The pilot had to find an area of thick growth so there were no large gaps in the foliage under the canopy. That wasn't hard to find in this unbroken rainforest. The center was reinforced for a landing place for the flitter.

Karvar launched the base from a hundred yards up. The package snapped open and a large mesh circle floated down to rest on top of the trees. It was colored in shades of green with a circle in the center in deeper shade. Karvar lowered the flitter toward the center.

Brielle squeezed her eyes shut. "I can't watch."

Karvar laughed. "It will hold the flitter. It's engineered that way."

It did hold, they came to a stop. Karvar employed the locks that fastened the flitter to the parking site.

"That was easy. Nice when something works."

"Yes!" Brielle reached across the small cabin and gave him a hug. For a moment his heart ratcheted up.

Brielle let go of him before he could pull her tighter and slid between the seats to the back of the flitter to the small hygenie.

He was a bit of an idiot where his wife was concerned, Karvar concluded as he set about powering down the ship. He'd have to watch himself. No point in raising expectations when this marriage would end once they were back in the New Prague Dome.

By his calculations, they had two hours of power left. The solar receptors would have them to full power four hours after sunrise, at the latest. "We'll leave for the old station in late morning. That way we'll be completely charged and well rested."

"My breather has three hours left." He checked Brielle's, which was the same, then did an air quality test. "The pollen level is only at six. On this system, we need filtered air when it reaches ten. I think you could go out without one. And the ship has a good filter system so we can always go inside. We'll keep an eye on the count as the afternoon goes on. That way we can save the breathers for times or locations that have high levels."

Brielle smiled at him, showing her dimples. "I can set an alarm. It will go off when it reaches nine."

"I think we should cut some limbs and cover the ship. Then from above, we'll be disguised."

"Karvar, you don't have to do that. There's a cover attached to the base. I read about it while you were finding a drop site. We just unroll it over the ship. It was made from camouflage so it's easier to observe animals."

"Well, that is good news." They got out and found the cover, more mesh colored to blend into the trees, with some leaf shapes attached. Within minutes they had the ship covered and explored the rest of the base. Several small tent areas plus some folding tables, circled the rim of the base. The tents and built-in tables and chairs were all made of mesh and thin metal rods were meant to pop up and later fold down for storage. The edge of the base had a four-foot high fence to keep the scientists from accidentally falling off. There were openings where rope or other ladders could be lowered if one wanted to go into the forest, and there were clear windows for looking into the woods underneath them.

"Cooking stations, work tables. Maybe crew quarters, too, though I wouldn't want to sleep with just mesh between me and a jungle animal," said Karvar.

"Maybe they had a force field for night time."

Karvar nodded. "Makes sense."

They walked for a while around the base, enjoying the springy sensation and peering down into the forest below them, watching birds and climbing animals.

Karvar yawned. "We should head back, make an early night."

Back in the flitter they ate a meal bar and arranged the back bench seat into a convertible bed. "I'll sleep in the driver's seat. It reclines," Karvar said. "Are you warm enough?"

"Yes. Do you think it will get stuffy in here?"

"I can open an access and run the filter. It won't use much energy." Karvar turned on the filter. The aromas of the jungle, mud, crushed leaves, a faint whiff of flowers filled the cabin. The trillers left her hair and fluttered toward the window.

"I'll let them out for a while. They probably want to eat."

"I hope Lila comes back." Brielle sounded worried but also sleepy. Her eyes drifted shut, thick dark crescents of lashes against her creamy skin.

"You can call for her later."

She nodded, not bothering to open her eyes.

Karvar watched as she slept. Someone wanted her dead. Somehow, she must have knowledge of who it was. Whoever it was a part of her life for many years. And they had powerful military ties. A traitor. They were afraid she would realize who the traitor was. He suspected the drug had a memory suppressant, but now that she was drug-free, memories could return.

Three days until he could contact Kyler and Mother...three days living in the flitter. It had seemed like an adequate situation when they made the plan to hide at the station. They had adequate supplies, Brielle was physically on the mend...

Good thing Brielle had spent so much time studying the rainforest. She had information he had no clue about, like those mud salps.

The breathers were the worst part. He'd probably be all right for a week or two on unfiltered air. But Brielle. Her lungs and heart had both been compromised by the drugs she'd been addicted to. Her treatment at this point was restorative, building up those organs. She needed good food too, while all they had were protein bars and not many of them.

He sighed. Kellac told tales of how he and Gema caught fish and ate bugs, during their stint on the Wilderness Survival show... Karvar had secretly shuddered at the idea. He liked good food, was a bit of a gourmet cook... He didn't see himself roasting insects on a stick.

He snorted. Somehow he could see Brielle doing it, with a grin.

Chapter Three

LILA AND THE OTHER trillers woke Karvar in the night, their tapping against the mesh covering the window waking him after a few hours sleep. He opened the access to let her and her buddies into the flitter. It was raining steadily now. Brielle would be happy to see the triller had returned.

I wonder just how smart those trillers are? He'd seen them around the dome but assumed they were insects. But Lila and the trillers attacked the drone...they'd distracted it and probably saved their lives. Like little watchdogs.

Karvar rolled onto his side to sleep. From this direction, he could see Brielle, on her back with her dark hair spread around her, the trillers resting lightly in her hair. She looked peaceful, despite their circumstances. Probably any circumstances where better now, knowing she wasn't going to die of a drug interaction.

While he had been worried and fearful for his brothers when they were in danger, his own life had been calm. Lab work, reports, technical discussions with colleagues... nothing life-threatening. Until now. Of the two of them, he was the more unsettled one.

Brielle...He was more at ease with her than he had been since the wedding night. Somehow the anger and embarrassment he'd felt when he found out about the drugs had evaporated. Brielle wasn't to blame for the secrecy about her drug addiction. Not really, though part of him wished she'd confided in him. Their relationship had been very shallow, he saw that now. He had not pushed for more intimacy, and Brielle had a secret so she hadn't either.

LILA AND THE TRILLERS woke Karvar and Brielle while it was still night. Above them, through the mesh cover, he saw bright lights. Not close. High and far away. *Looking for us?* He wondered if they knew the flitter was missing and hoped they didn't read heat signatures, or if they did, there were enough sizeable beasts in this area to confuse their readings.

"The ship?" Brielle asked.

"Yes. Looking for movement, I think."

They watched the lights get farther away.

"They are pretty confident they already killed us," Karvar said. "They are just going through the motions, probably to please someone higher up with exacting standards. If they knew the flitter was missing, they could have found us by now."

"What do you mean?"

"Ship like that, with a trained crew...they should have found us. So this crew may be ex-military, Low level or not trained well."

She was silent for a while, stroking Lila with one finger. "Or out of practice. Someone who works in an office with a com."

Karvar was surprised at her insight. "You're right. Someone out of their element. That might give us a clue."

"Could you tell if the ship was from the New Prague Protectorate?"

"Not really. It was built here on New Prague. The drones are our model, too. But not the latest. More like models we would refurbish and sell to an outlying planet. A decade out of date."

She shrugged. "No epiphany, here. I've tried to find out in the past who kidnapped me."

"So you never met anyone?"

"Only the first time, when I was kidnapped and drugged. There was a man who eventually took me back to school, but he was disguised and didn't speak to me. All my other contacts have been through my old armcom, and your father has that. I've had no messages on this new com. Hopefully, Kyler's researchers will be able to find some clues from it. Or maybe I'll recall something useful, but in all these years that hasn't happened."

She yawned. It had started raining again, the gentle patter on the roof was comforting.

"Don't be offended...but could your drugger be on your father's staff?

She didn't look at him. "Or my father?"

"Yeah. I know it's shocking... but so few knew where we would be. My mother and father, Kyler. I doubt Skyleen even knows. Kellac and Kaistril knew we were going into hiding, but they didn't know where."

"I didn't tell anyone. I couldn't because when I woke in the hospital my com had been taken off. Kyler didn't want to let anyone know since there was a security breach, so I didn't even talk to my father. Are you sure my dad knew about my collapse?"

"Yes, my mother thought he should know. But she didn't tell him we were going anywhere, just that you had fallen ill and we would keep him informed. We didn't tell him until the next day after your sisters had left for camp."

"Then Kyler told me your father was informed we were able to leave for our honeymoon a couple days late."

"Did they find drugs in my luggage?"

Karvar nodded. "They did, and have questioned anyone who had access to your suite. Everyone thinks all is normal."

Brielle sat back and tilted her head so she could see out of the window. "I rarely saw my father once I went to school on Terra, so most of his staff are strangers to me. He didn't like us to visit the office, I doubt I have been there in ten years. I spent short vacation times on Terra most years and joined my sisters on a planned long vacation once a year. My father rarely came to those, we had nannies and tutors to care for us. Mostly we messaged." She leaned her head back against the seat. "We weren't close, not like your family."

"And your mother is on Chen Chen."

Brielle shrugged. "Maybe. She left when I was six. I never once heard from her."

"You didn't spend part of your childhood with your mother?" He hadn't known that. Most children who had unmarried parents traveled between the two.

"No. Dad remarried when I turned eight. He traveled a lot."

"It might not be him or his staff... but who would know where we were? Or would be able to get the information? Coyt and Loyt flew us down here, there is no way they would betray Kyler. And I wouldn't want to try to mess with them to get information. They are kind of scary."

"And why would they want to kill me? For money, I guess. Seriously, I don't know who it is."

"They think you'll remember now that you aren't drugged."

"I don't think it affected my memory so much. Well, when it was time for a fix, I'd get agitated, which made it hard to think...Glad I don't have that sensation anymore."

She yawned. "We can sleep in, can't we?"

"Sure. But could you beam the station files to my com? I didn't download them."

Brielle sent him the data, then curled back up on the bed to sleep. She wished she could stay awake, to keep the conversation going. It was the most they had spoken to each other since before their wedding...but she was so tired. Like her bones were sinking down to the floor, holding her down. Brielle sighed and closed her eyes. She was tired and needed to sleep, not obsess.

She woke to sun. Karvar had pulled the mesh covering from the flitter and delicious heat warmed her shoulders and back. She peeked, Karvar was sitting up in his seat, reading something on his com. His hair was mussed. He looked sexy like that.

Who knew what the next few days would bring? Hopefully, she would be functional, even helpful. What a burden she must seem to him. Drug-addled, ill, dragging his life down with incessant physical demands. A security breach, too, and a secret keeper. Not a full partner. Not a wife.

Half asleep, she dared to daydream a little. What if she was well? Competent, not a sickly burden. Able to carve something meaningful from life, rather than skulking around for information to give to her handler?

There wasn't time for her to redeem herself with Karvar, she knew that. She could have told him…she should have told him rather than lie. But she's been watched, all the time. Maybe they would have just died sooner, if her handler learned she had told Karvar. Or her sisters…they might have been hurt or killed.

By the time she was well enough to start thinking about ways she could contribute in life, their marriage would be over. It would be over right now, except for the threat to her life. Karvar, being a decent man, had chosen to see this drug treatment through. And now there were more issues… a traitor somewhere.

A silky fuzz bundle prodded at her hair. The trillers liked to slide underneath her hair, out of the light. She lifted her hair a little and the trillers slid to her neck, safe in the dark of her hair.

"Did I sleep long?"

Karvar glanced at her with a slight smile. "Long enough for the ship to charge. Why don't you grab some food and we'll head for Glim Falls? I found the coordinates."

The trillers climbed out from under her hair as she brushed it and fluttered around the window. Karvar opened it and they flew out.

"Oh. You aren't planning to leave before they come back are you?"

Karvar grinned. "I can wait. It is not like we have any kind of schedule we have to follow."

The trillers returned in a half hour or so, which gave Brielle time to eat and get cleaned up in the tiny hygenie.

They flew throughout the afternoon. In late afternoon they spotted the Glim Falls station, a squat metal building surrounded by thick growth.

The trillers struggled out from under her hair and began an agitated flight toward the window, tapping it.

"Maybe they are hungry," Karvar said.

She watched for a moment, feeling more and more anxious. "I don't know...they haven't done this before. Except at the pool, with the drone.s And last night with the ship."

Karvar slowly lowered the flitter to avoid thick vines and trees in the forest. "Maybe we are going into a trap. I'm finding some thick growth—just in case."

Brielle pulled up the ship holo and expanded it so they could see the exterior of the ship better.

A glint of metal. "Oh," she cried. "A drone. Above us."

Karvar put them into a steep dive so that the restraints tightened, constricting her breathing. They landed with a jerk into thick vines. He inched the ship into a stand of bushes and trees. Brielle looked with dismay at the dark goo that reached the window. They were in a pool of mud. "Karvar."

"Quiet now," he breathed.

There was a strange sucking sound. The rear of the ship rocked, then upended so they were only kept from crashing down into the flight console by their mesh restraints. Brielle twisted around in her seat to see what was moving the flitter and stifled a scream. A huge worm-like beast, brown like the mud they were hiding in, rose up out of the ooze. Its mouth opened showing a large hole surrounded by triangular teeth and a fuzzy tongue. A deep rumbling roar sounded.

"Salp," Brielle said in a high pitched voice. "Didn't know they roared."

It loomed over them, hitting the flitter with its huge, knobby head, shoving them deeper into the curtain of vines they were hiding under.

The flitter swerved sideways and they landed with a thump, resting against a tree trunk. "Well, that wasn't so bad," Karvar whispered. "Better than I would have dared hide it." They were deep under thick growth, barely able to see out of the flitter's windows due to the thick ferns and leaves surrounding them.

The drone, lights glinting in the gloom of the forest, whipped by. The mud beast lunged at it, opening its maw from which a long feathery tongue emerged. The tongue snapped out at the drone, surrounding it, and pulled it rapidly into the wide mouth. The mud beast swallowed it.

Inside the body of the beast, the lights of the drone continued to blink, showing through the mud-colored, translucent skin. The beast writhed, plunged into the muck, then rose back up, the force of its movements causing the flitter to scrape against the bark of the trees. Karvar started the ship, elevating out of the danger and farther into the forest from the mud pool. The beast circled around toward them, mouth open.

"Our ship is too big to swallow," Brielle cried, her eye glued to the holo. "I hope."

The way forward was blocked by tree trunks.

Karvar grabbed her arm. "Brace yourself. I think it can still reach us."

It struck, slamming the flitter with such force they were flung into a tree nearly as wide as the ship. There was a scrape of metal, the crunching roar of breaking view glass and metal. Brielle screamed as pieces of debris hurtled through the small ship.

They stopped with a thud.

Brielle gasped for breath. Her restraints were so tight she could barely breathe. Her ribs hurt, her neck... she felt a warm trickle slide down her neck.

"I have a cut, need the kit." She undid her harness and got up to crawl to the back.

The flitter rocked as the mud salp flung itself toward them.

"Watch out!" Karvar grabbed Brielle and she flopped against him, held tight. He was still harnessed. After a little while the salp stopped punching the ship. "Let me get a little farther away before you try to get back there." He dumped her back into her seat and she harnessed.

He inched them backwards and then backed into an opening, pointing the front toward the salp. "I think we're out of reach here."

He nimbly unharnessed and grabbed the med kit. He cleaned the scratch with a disposable pad and spread some new skin over the wound on her temple. Then they looked to see what was happening with the salp. It was no longer trying to bash the ship, now it was flinging itself into the pool and then up into the air.

"We're lucky we didn't crash. That thing must be twice the weight of our ship." Karvar's hand absently caressed her back. "I can see why the journals caution against flying low."

They watched the animal. The salp returned with more vigor, thrashing around and flinging mud everywhere. Karvar started the flitter but getting out of the thick growth broke their window even more. They hastily pulled on their breathers as humid air wafted through the broken window.

"The drone's lights are off now," Brielle told Karvar, as he concentrated at making a path through the thick trees that avoided the mud pool. "And I think it is further up the throat. Well, the salp is all throat. But now I think it is just a meter down."

Karvar paused his wrestling with the controls and looked at her holo. "You're right. I wonder if the salp will eject it."

They watched the salp plunge into the muddy water, then fling itself into the air, occasionally rushing toward their ship. The drone was definitely moving up the throat.

Karvar got the flitter into a small clearing and landed. "I want it. When it spits it out. I'd like to examine it. Might be able to get some data to Kyler when we can communicate."

"You mean, go out there? With that monster crashing around?"

"Yes. You hold the laser on it while I get its attention. I don't want the drone to land in the mud. With any luck, it will spit it out here on solid ground."

It didn't sound like a great idea. "You really think it might help figure out who's trying to kill us?"

"Yes, it will have all types of data. Clues." He opened the door and glanced around. "I doubt there are any predators around with all the noise that thing is making." The salp struck toward the ship, which was several yards out of its reach.

"But look how fast it can move, Karvar, it just wouldn't be safe."

"Look! The drone is almost to the mouth opening. I can stay right by the flitter. I'll jump and yell so I have its attention. You'll hold the laser."

Brielle stared at him as he made pleading eyes at her. "All right." She shook her head. "But I officially state I think this is crazy."

They climbed out and Karvar gave her a quick refresher on the laser and made sure it was set to stun. She stood to one side so she wouldn't accidentally stun him if she fired and he shouted and jumped up and down.

The salp whipped around toward Karvar so fast Brielle screamed and jumped, nearly dropping the laser.

"Careful with that laser!"

"Right." She pulled it back up and took a wide-legged stance, aiming the weapon toward the salp. The drone was still moving up its gullet.

"It stinks." Through the breather the scent of mold and a sulphur-stench reached her. Something else too, the smell she recognized as fertilizer.

"Here we go!" Karvar shouted.

He was having fun, she realized. His color was high, eyes bright.

The salp shot out a gush of foul-smelling liquid and partially digested matter, ejecting the drone with enough force it flew the few yards toward them. The drone clanked on the ground as a stream of foul liquid splattered over them. Brielle screamed in disgust.

Karvar laughed and cried, "Shoot it, shoot!"

She shot, though her hands were slimy with salp vomit. The salp reared back and flopped into the mud pool, dousing them once again. Karvar leaped to the drone, grabbed it and pulled it back while she shot at the salp in the mud. It disappeared. Laughing, Karvar took the laser from her, turning it off. "We're good."

She stared at him, aghast. "Good? Good?" She lifted up a lock of salp-vomit filled hair. "You call this good?"

Karvar leaped up past her and grabbed the toolkit. "I'm just going to make sure it's disabled. I'll take it apart once we set up camp."

Brielle noticed he barely had any salp vomit, while she was soaked with it, and with no shower, either. Her hair was also stiff with dried blood from the cut. She sat on the footstep of the flitter, not wanting to get salp vomit all over the interior. Karvar took some pieces off the drone and messed around with whatever was inside. It seemed to take forever until she heard the thud of the drone pieces being stowed away and Karvar came around to the door, smiling and handsome.

"Why don't you cover my seat with a blanket so I don't get it too messy," she said. He did so, cheerfully. She climbed in and flopped into her seat. The salp vomit was drying. Brielle managed to clean her hands, but her suit was a disgusting mess, and her hair needed a water rinse to be clean. At least the breather had kept the vomit off her face. Out of her mouth.

"Hey look. The window has a self-repair function. Wasn't expecting that." Karvar looked happy and relaxed.

Even the trillers would have nothing to do with her, they were lined up against the window.

Karvar hopped into his seat and started the engine. "Well, Glim Falls is out, they were expecting us there. Where to now?"

She gave him a narrowed-eyed glance. "Head for rain clouds."

Chapter Four

IT RAINED MOST LATE afternoons in the forest, so it didn't take long to find a bank of clouds. Karvar launched the base and landed the flitter. They got out into warm, fat raindrops that soaked through their coveralls in moments.

"I'm going around to the side to scrub the vomit out," Brielle said and disappeared.

Karvar did the same, stripping in the warm rain and tossing his coverall to the floor.

The rain increased, and he relished the pounding sensation on his shoulders. It felt good to be free, in the open air.

He was very conscious that right on the other side of the flitter Brielle was washing off, nude in the rain. The rain increased again, becoming a real gusher. He laughed, ducking his head to keep water out of his nose. The mesh floor of the base was too tight a weave to keep up with the intensity of the rain, soon water was up to his ankles. He supposed there was nothing to be concerned about; the base was built for this environment, after all.

A squeal and a splash came from the other side. "Brielle?" He rushed around the flitter to make sure she was all right. The base, covered with water, was horribly slippery, and he skidded toward where Brielle was on the floor and landed on his ass, bouncing a little, crashing into her.

Brielle struggled to sit up, pushing her soaked hair away from her face. She gained a bit of weight, just enough to make every inch of her perfectly smooth, even more exquisite than the glimpse he'd had of her wearing the lacy gown on their wedding night.

He couldn't stop looking, and he couldn't stop the erection that rose.

She squeaked and grabbed her coveralls and covered up. "Karvar!"

"I thought you might be hurt."

"I fell, but I am not hurt."

"Right. It's slippery." Those words reminded him even more of hot sex. The good thing for all the rain obscuring their vision or she'd see him blush.

"Well, I'll go back over to my side and scrub my clothes." He slipped as he tried to stand, took two steps and landed on his ass again.

She giggled.

He half turned, noticing she was not holding her coverall so that it covered all of her nude flesh. He could see one breast completely, and it was exquisite.

He deliberately bounced on the mesh floor and she lost her balance, landing with a splash. She also lost her cover-up.

"Why, you!" She threw her still disgusting coverall at him.

He ducked it and one armed a big handful of water at her, splashing her on the shoulder. She retaliated with a swoosh of her own and then the battle was on. Splashing turned to kicking. Karvar tried to stand to kick water more effectively, but the floor was still so slippery he crashed, landing with his chest on her silky legs.

"Oh, yes!" Karvar yelled. Brielle splashed him as fast and hard as she could. He got closer, intending to dunk her face in the now six-inch puddle. She kicked and splashed, grabbed his shoulders as if to try and duck him.

BRIELLE LAUGHED SO hard her stomach muscles cramped. Karvar was half on top of her, laughing as hard as she was. Stars he was handsome when he smiled, bright eyed, gleaming white teeth.

His skin against hers felt hot and smooth. Her breasts were smashed against his chest.

Naked.

Suddenly they were not laughing, but breathing hard. Then he kissed her. His lips were firm, cool from the water, but his tongue was hot, hungry, thrusting into her mouth. She met it with her own stokes, desire replacing the amusement, making her legs feel heavy. She'd seen his arousal while they played and stored the sight as a secret memory to be examined later, when she was alone again. Now she felt it, so hard, so smooth against her hip... His arms pulled her tighter and now she was half sitting in his lap.

It would be so good. *Wait. Are we ready for this?* The thought screamed in her mind, but his lips left her mouth. He hoisted her up just enough that her nipple was at his mouth and with a groan, she sank her hands into his thick hair and rubbed her nipple against his lips, caution tossed away. *I want this, I'm going to have him.* His mouth captured her, tugging and rubbing his tongue over the tip, sending waves of pleasure straight to her pussy.

Karvar devoured her other nipple and then lowered her, sliding her down his chest, his mouth moving into new territory before reaching her lips once again. Then more kisses, with his rain-slick hands running up and down her back, cupping her bottom, sliding up to her breasts. Brielle reveled in his touch, a feast for her senses, making her hot and shivery at the same time.

His cock was hard, thrusting up behind her buttocks. She teased him, swaying side to side. Karvar groaned and held her face between both hands, kissing her hard.

Brielle spread her legs wider, her knees on either side of his legs. She raised up and slipped a hand between them to his cock and then she had him at her entrance. He was still, mouth against her, panting against her lips, but not kissing her. Waiting, letting her move things forward. He held her tight and she could feel the thundering of his heart against her chest. She leaned back a little and stared into his eyes as she lowered onto him, his hands now cupping her buttocks, holding her steady.

"Oh." He was so large, she wasn't sure this would work, but she wanted him. Wanted this much of him to store in her memories. Slowly she slid down his straining erection until she stopped, filled almost to bursting. They kissed, a deep, intense meeting of their tongues, and as they kissed liquid heated sizzled through her veins, settling deep between her legs where he joined her. Karvar thrust his hips, not hard, just ...enough. She groaned as pleasure radiated from inside. He gripped her hips in his large hands and took over the business of moving her, finding a rhythm unique to the two of them. She caught on and he freed a hand so his fingers circled her swollen clit as they thrust together harder and faster, heated moves, turning into a quest. They moved faster, both desperate for completion.

"Soon," she gasped out.

"Yes." His hands clamped on her hips, moving her up and down his shaft, harder and faster than she could do on her own, Brielle fell into a vortex of need, anticipation building within and then the powerful, delicious wave swept through her as Karvar shouted and thrust into her as deep as he could.

The rain was a light drizzle, pattering gently on them, a soft drumming on the hull of the ship. Brielle was so limp in his arms Karvar wasn't sure she was conscious.

"Let's get you out of the rain." He stood, pulling her up, steadying her as she wobbled. "Easy now." He half supported her into the ship and placed her on the nearest seat while he moved to the back and rearranged the seat back into the bed.

"You get some rest. Here. Drink some water and eat something. I'll get our suits washed and toss them into the back to dry."

"Thanks." He wrapped her up in the heat blanket and she forced herself to drink the water and eat part of the meal bar while he went outside to finished washing their coveralls

We had sex. Right here in the open, in the rain. I didn't see anything like that coming. We went from nothing to...everything.

KARVAR TRIED TO MAKE sense of it. He wasn't an impulsive person. He'd been trying to ignore his attraction to her, and she certainly hadn't acted as though she had sexual feelings for him.

He hoped she was all right. She had been so tight, she might be sore now. He hadn't had much restraint.

She could have been a virgin. He stopped scrubbing the coveralls in his hands, stunned at the thought. What did he know about her? She was young, just out of University, and she'd spent her years trying to get through college while on an addicting drug. Brielle had told him more than once she spent all her time in University studying. He knew she had no crowd of friends on New Prague like Kyler's kids had, to run around with. A loner. She'd managed to graduate with two degrees, while drugged.

It was entirely possible that had been her first time. She hadn't acted as though there was any pain, though.

The rain had stopped, the water accumulation was now draining off the floor of the camp. He wrung out the excess water from the coveralls and carried them into the flitter, holding them low and in front as he entered. Somehow, he felt awkward about nudity now.

Brielle was asleep, the half-eaten meal bar in her hand. She had shadows under her eyes. The past days had not been easy for her, and now she was looking more fragile. She needed rest, not a complicated affair with a husband who was not likely to stay in the marriage. He slid past her and spread the clothing to dry. He wrapped in a blanket and took a little nap himself.

He woke to late afternoon sun. Their coveralls were already dry so he dressed. Karvar left Brielle asleep in the flitter and went out to the base. The rain had moved on. He opened up one of the tent areas on the base, one with a pop-up worktable. It was still light out since the clouds had blown away, he'd spend some time working on the drone.

Work was always calming.

He took the drone apart listening to the whistles and calls of birds and animals living in the trees just underneath them. It was relaxing. *Soothing.*

Why did he need to be soothed? Having sex didn't mean any disaster was imminent. They'd go on just as planned. Get in communication with Kyler, get back to the palace. Make sure Brielle was healthy, then make arrangements to quietly end the marriage. He'd make sure she had a good settlement and of course he would make sure she was safe. He wasn't angry with her, he wanted her to have a good life. But he learned the lesson his brothers had tried to cram into his head and heart—he should marry for love, someone he was truly compatible with.

The sex had been amazing. He wasn't the wild type, not like Kaistril who had been a bit of a lady's man before he got turned into a cyborg. He had girlfriends, companions, lovers, though not much the past few years, with all the commotion and extra work caused by the war. But maybe his love life had been a little predictable. Ordinary.

Not with Brielle. She was in the fantasy sex realm.

He worked until the sun dipped low. Even on the base it probably wasn't wise to be outdoors in the forest at night when predators started to hunt. He closed up the workplace and joined Brielle in the flitter.

She'd woken up at some point and pulled on her coverall, but now she was fast asleep again in the fading light.

He took his time looking at her. What was it about her? All Puregen women were aesthetically pleasing to look at. That was a big part of choosing a Puregen child, determining their characteristics. She had a perfect figure, flawless skin. It had felt smoother than silk under his fingers. His hands remembered the size and texture of her buttocks, her breasts. This wasn't Puregen bioengineering. Sure, her parents had chosen a certain look, dark hair and light eyes were still popular on New Prague. Heck, most of the New Prague Puregen society looked like siblings. Brielle had some unidentifiable extra, something that couldn't be made in a lab. Damned if he knew what it was,

He ate a meal bar and made himself settle down to sleep.

BRIELLE WOKE A LITTLE before sunrise. She'd basically slept from yesterday afternoon clear through until morning. The drone, the salp, making love, exhaustion.

Making love. It wasn't really that. Just sex. Amazing sex that had flared up out of nowhere.

Did he know it had been her first time? She had closed herself off from friendships, lovers. Life dealing with the drug and the demands of her handler who wanted to impress her with their power had taken all her wits. She looked wistfully at the time on young couples, wondering what it would be like to have such a relationship— but such relationships were not for her.

Her hope in marrying Karvar had been that she would have access to medical care and also the protection of the Protectorate family. That proved true. She was now drug-free, though her overall health was not normal, not yet. Maybe not ever.

But she felt passion. That was a sign of health. His hands, those kisses, the sensation of him inside her... it brought a rich awareness she couldn't ignore. She'd like to do it again. She quietly used the hygenie and made a cup of tea, deep in thought.

Karvar was asleep in the recliner, his arm flung above his head. She leaned over him to open the window for the trillers, who had figured out how to get under the camouflage mesh covering the ship. She moved slowly, hoping not to wake him, but his eyes popped open as the trillers fluttered inside.

"Sorry, didn't mean to wake you," she whispered. His eyes, that rare honey color, were lit up by the rising sun; they had an otherworldly look, surrounded by his thick dark lashes.

"Come here," he whispered. The huskiness of his voice sent a thrill through her. She leaned into him, his hands slid up her arms to her hair, gliding through, making her secretly glad she'd brushed all the tangles out when she woke up.

He pulled her lips down to his. "I don't think there is any way of stopping this now the floodgates are open. I thought about it for a long time last night." He spoke softly and low against her lips, sending whisper thrills through her. She wrapped her arms around his neck.

"No, I think there is no going back."

"I HAVE THE DRONE IN one of the workstations. I'll pack it up. I thought we might fly. Not sure where, but away from here. But we could break early and set up camp. I'd like to look at the drone some more."

"All right." She followed Karvar toward the fence that circled the base to a tent. It had several wall pockets for belongings and a type of cot and a table made of taut mesh. The table was covered with drone pieces. Brielle helped him pack it back inside a bag.

They flew through the morning, with no evidence of drones or ships. Karvar found a suitable area and launched the base.

"Do you think we are safe here?"

"I can't be sure, but this is a huge forest, and we landed in a completely random place. They will expect us to try to follow the mountain pass down to the Recondin fields, I think. No way can we go over the mountains, we'd have to take one of the passes and there are only a few of them. It would be easy to watch the passes."

"I wonder if they actually know we're alive."

"I don't think they do. I think they could find us if they really felt like hunting us. They might be thinking there were some research scientists in the area, though."

"The com satellite will be here soon."

"Yes. I hope to have data from this drone to upload to them." He checked his com.

"We'll have to watch the pollen count and use the breathers if it gets high. The advantage of being up here is there is so much less pollen to breathe in."

She looked at the pollen count; it was safe right now.

"We'll need to stretch our food supply."

Brielle nodded. "I have data on local edible plants. The station crew did a lot of foraging and cooking as far as I could tell. It seemed to involve a lot of camaraderie."

It was time to take her medicine and she felt tired now.

"I think I'll take a little nap."

"Good idea."

Karvar was already opening the flitter storage and pulling out pieces of the drone.

Later Brielle woke after a deep nap to find Karvar fixing a meal. Her stomach growled. "I'm so glad you were able to grab the emergency rations. This would be so hard if we had to hunt food, too."

Karvar smiled at her and handed her a plate. Her trillers, who had found her while she slept, fluttered off to feed.

"How are you feeling?"

She blushed a little, not about to tell him she felt a tiny bit sensitive in certain places. "I'm fine, though I feel tired."

He nodded. "We've had a lot of activity the past couple days, and you should have been doing much more resting."

She nodded. He was right, she'd been active or tense for quite a bit of the last few days. But more than that it was all the changes. No drugs, the bombing, fleeing, the whole drone-rain-sex thing. The sex...and the change it could make in their relationship. She took in a deep breath, trying to ease some tension.

"Do I need to apologize for...?"

She couldn't look him in the eye. "Oh, no. I'm not upset. It was fun, playing in the rain, we'd been so tense. And this morning. No, it was just the heat of the moment."

Karvar nodded. "Yes, definitely heat." He finished his meal. "And you are right. I think the first time things lightened up at all for me was when we saw the salp swallow that drone. How could things get more absurd?"

Brielle was glad he changed the subject away from the sex. "Well, I think the salp vomit made everything more absurd. And gross."

"Followed by naked in the rain. Star gods." Karvar grinned at her and she loved how his eyes lit up. "Hopefully we will just have a calm little time here until we can get in contact with Kyler."

Karvar worked on the drone while she read and napped in the sun for a while. By the evening meal she was feeling more energetic.

"I can tell the lazy afternoon did you some good," Karvar said as they ate.

"I do feel better, and I spent quite a bit of time looking at reports on edible plants here. There are tons. The Big Poison Station Crew ate 'native' at least once a week and often competed to see who could prepare the tastiest dishes."

"We have all day tomorrow, the satellite won't be in range until middle of the night, so why don't we take the flitter into the forest and look for some of those plants? I have all the data I can get from the drone, so that project is finished. We don't have many cooking options, but maybe we could get something that doesn't need to cook. Or we could use that small flame pit and roast something over a fire, if we can find enough dry fuel."

"Oh. I read about fuel. There is a tree, you can pull off the outer bark and burn the inner bark, which peels off easily. I'll find that data."

"I guess I can use the laser to cut some wood. You might want to look that up, too." He laughed.

"What's so funny?"

"My brother Kellac met his wife on a wilderness world survivor program. A view-cast competition. I thought their wilderness experience was insane, yet here we are chopping wood and finding plants."

They entered the forest the next morning after packing up camp.

"I have an elevation map pulled up. We want to go here," she showed him the hologram. "There are fruits and plants, plus we won't be in danger of salps in the mud pools."

Karvar studied the map and flew carefully and as slowly as possible while Brielle search for trees and fruits she marked.

"There." Brielle spotted a stand of a type of fruit somewhat like a plantain. Long purple and brown speckled fruits hung together in clusters.

"Those are Prague Plantians."

"You could use the small laser. I can hover, you open the window and cut?"

"All right."

He pulled up to the tree and she climbed up on the seat and leaned out the window a bit to cut the bunch. It was heavier than she expected and she flopped back onto her seat with the large bunch in her lap.

"So what do they taste like?" Karvar asked.

"Supposed to be sweet." Brielle unpeeled one oblong fruit, revealing a pale pink mushy fruit with tiny dark seeds. She broke it in half and handed Karvar a piece.

"That is tasty." The fruit had a sweet, almost creamy flavor with just a hint of tartness. "I'm glad we got that big bunch."

They found a dull green globe-shaped citrus fruit about an hour later. "Those are melontains. They taste like a mix of citrus and melon and are juicy."

"Sound good." Since they were growing on a short tree on the edge of a clearing, Karvar landed the ship on the ground. "I'll go get the fruit, but you watch out for animals."

"All right." Brielle felt less certain about this, but the reports she'd read about harvesting fruits did mention that the wildlife rushed away when they heard the ships land. Karvar was able to reach the fruits and easily cut down half a dozen, carrying them in one of the cooking pots.

"That went well, don't you think?" He asked as he climbed back into the flitter. Brielle placed the weapon back in its secure holder.

"It did, but I'll be glad when we can stop doing things that make my heart race."

"Really?" He waggled his eyebrows at her and she burst out laughing.

"I meant with fear, Karvar. Not that! Heart racing of that nature is beneficial."She grabbed one of the green fruits and started peeling it.

"Maybe after we set camp we can explore that."

The heated look he gave her made her breath hitch. She placed the fruit on the floor at her feet. "Why wait until then?"

Karvar turned from the controls, eyes wide. "You're right. Why wait? The only thing we have to do is contact the satellite." His hands left the controls and he unharnessed, while she did the same. He climbed to the back seat first, then pulled her to his lap as she moved to the back."You have the best ideas," He said as his lips found hers a deep kiss.

THAT EVENING AS SHE crawled onto the back bed, she looked at Karvar, and patted the bed. "I think we can share. You could stretch out better."

The grin he gave her was wicked. "It's not the stretching out that interests me."

He climbed back to the bed and kissed her. "I really don't think we need these coveralls," he whispered in her ear, so she sat up and took off her clothes while he watched.

"You are so very lovely,"

"Oh, all Puregen girls are lovely."

He shrugged, "I guess. I think you are particularly beautiful, but maybe it is just personal preference."

"Well, it is kind of you to say."

"Hmm. I think you don't believe me." Karvar sat up and pulled off his suit, tossing it to the front seat where he'd slept the night before. Then he turned and tackled her to the bed and she reacted with wild giggle. "I guess I will just have to show you."

"Yes, show me. I need a lot of convincing."

Chapter Five

BRIELLE WOKE IN THE night, hot and sweaty. It had rained during the evening and the temperature had risen due to humidity. Her coverall was making her crazy.

They had found several lab coats with pockets in a small cupboard. If she altered her coverall, she could always put a lab coat over it if she got chilly. There were some extra large coveralls she could make do with if she needed to. And how did anyone get cold in the jungle? Even after being in the rain, she had shivered out of reaction to having sex and exhaustion, not chilly weather. She slid around to the cupboard section and found the cutter in the first aid kit.

Karvar was still deeply asleep. She slipped out of her suit and used the cutter to scoop out the neckline. She cut off the long sleeves and legs and put the coverall back on, pleased with the less confining garment.

It was good they had talked, Brielle didn't feel awkward around him, though she couldn't stop looking at him as he worked on the drone in the small work station. She couldn't stop thinking about sex.

Am I in love with him? Or is this lust? Maybe it was both. She didn't have experience with relationships. She hadn't had a boyfriend back in school. Back then, friends talked with each other and learned to unravel their feelings. That would be nice, to have friends to talk to.

Sexual desire was a big part, and that was new to her since the drug was out of her system. It had suppressed her normal libido, which hadn't bothered her back in school. One less thing to worry about.

Karvar's alarm went off for the middle of the night satellite connection, and he pulled up his holo. "The satellite should be accessible for the next few hours." They watched the com for the connection.

"It's time," he said. She rolled onto her side and watched him in the dim light from the computer as he tapped his information into it. "Karvar reporting. May Day. These are our current coordinates." He gave a string of numbers.

She waited for the reply. No reply came. Karvar tried again, several times.

"Something's wrong. I'm going to look at the equipment." Karvar pulled on his coverall, grabbed the flitter tool kit and leaped out.

Brielle snatched up their breathers and followed him. "Pollen counts are up," she said.

It took a while to check the equipment. "Everything looks fine," he said. He opened the hologram from his armcom and tried again. Nothing.

There was a flicker of movement on the far side of the base. Brielle jumped. She grabbed Karvar and hauled him into the flitter just as a nightglider floated onto the base from over the edge, helped by its tear-drop shaped transparent, double wings. It had thousands of appendages and dozens of rows of sharp teeth. Karvar realized at the last minute what was happening and slammed the door shut. The nightglider flew to the flitter. Its multiple eyes were blank, soulless. Brielle shivered, seeing the teeth up close.

"Gods, I'm so sorry. I wasn't thinking. Should have had the laser."

"Yes." They sat there silently until their breathing finally slowed.

"Something happened to the satellite," Brielle said, holding back tears. Still no way to communicate.

"Yes."

"So we need a new plan."

Karvar got the blaster and opened the door. "I think we need to pack up and go. In case our coordinates were overheard."

She held the laser while Karvar cleared off the work area he'd set the drone out on. Once it was stowed he released the anchors on the flitter and retracted the base. Then they took off in the dark, flying just above the trees, changing course frequently, random. They didn't speak as he flew just above the dark forest. Brielle tried to stay alert, to watch for a ship or drones, but her eyes kept drooping.

"I'm sorry, Karvar. I can't seem to stay awake."

"That's all right. I think I'll just fly for an hour or so, then launch the base." He paused. "You have your trillers, right?"

"Oh, yes. They came back when that nightglider showed up."

"Good. That thing was larger than I expected. All right. I'm sure they are all fine, at the palace. Someone was able to shut down the satellite, is all."

"I hope they are all fine,"

"We'll try to connect tonight, also. Day one, two and three try to connect, then wait six days. That's the schedule if we miss connecting."

"All right."

She slept most of the day, but Karvar did fly into the forest for an hour or so to look for edible plants. In the late afternoon Karvar launched the base.

"We've flown a long way. I can see the mountains to the south," Brielle said as he checked the com once again.

"We flew nine hours, so the ship will need to recharge for a long time. There won't be enough light to recharge for long today."

While the ship charged Karvar started some type of project at the big work table on the base. "The drone had a couple stunners. I'm removing them and soon we'll have two handhelds. If the contact doesn't work out tonight I'll finish those small stunners so we can catch some jumpers you mentioned the station crew eating."

"There is a lot of information on cooking jumpers. And there are some spices and salt in the ration box you grabbed."

He shook his head back and forth. "I swear I feel like I am reliving my brother Kellac's wilderness adventure."

"They were players in some kind of contest, right?"

"Yes. They were dumped on a wilderness planet and followed by cameras. But the Gorvas invaded using an unknown jumpstream in their vicinity. The Gorvas were headed toward Toph and Adelphia, in the same system. They had jumpstream maps we sure didn't know about. Took out the View-cast ship, then headed for Toph. Mom kept saying Kellac and the girl would be all right—this was before we knew Gema—and she was right. We sent ships to Toph and Adelphia but we were too late. It will take them decades to recover, even with Alliance help. They had been devastated, most of the population either killed or taken for cyborg processing. Kellac and Gema on Farradae were fine, though Gema was in a bad accident Farradae healers were able to help her.."

"And now they live there on Farradae? They have the twins." Gema was a warm person, both in appearance with her gold-streaked hair and in manner.

"The twins of destruction, " Karvar grinned. "Yes. Those boys are a handful. Good thing they live out in the middle of nowhere raising cattle."

"My little sisters are with them."

"Yes, but I think Gema took the kids down to the Zh Cle' settlement, into the forest. There are lots of other kids. I'm sure they are having a great time. Probably less structured than they would have at camp."

Brielle laughed. "Then they probably don't know what to do with themselves. Unstructured time is not part of my father's parenting plan."

Karvar nodded. "I see that in many Puregen families. My parents would take us to a farm on Chen Chen, inland, not the touristy area. That was great. No one knew who we were. We ran wild. But back in New Prague we were pretty structured with school and activities."

"I can see how being on a farm that was pleasant for your family."

THE CONNECTION DIDN'T work again that night. Karvar was silent, worried. "I'll fly a few hours away from here, just in case someone captured our signal location." They left the area and for an hour or so Brielle scanned the holo for signs of a drone or the ship, but the night was calm.

"You should go to bed. I'll fly for a couple more hours and then launch the base. If they haven't confronted us by now, I doubt they will."

Brielle dozed while he flew to a random location and launched the base in the dark. She woke briefly to let the trillers out.

"I'll wake when it is light and cover the ship with the camo net. No need to risk running into anything unfriendly tonight," he told her.

She nodded and slid over on the bed, making room for him.

"I'm not sure I can sleep," Karvar said.

"How about some music? We could listen until we feel sleepy. Or a book... I have a collection of old books." Brielle said.

"Music would be good."

She played a selection of strings and pipes, music he vaguely remembered from the wedding.

"Is that what we danced to?"

"Yes, the Stardust Waltz, played by the Chen Chen Chamber Players. I got to see them perform once in Paris, Terra. It was glorious."

"I should have mother invite them to New Prague for a performance." He shifted restlessly. "I don't know why we can't communicate."

"I doubt it is anything on our end that is going wrong, Karvar. It is something with the satellite."

"Yes. And by now Kyler has to know there is something wrong."

They were silent for a while. He sighed. "The pollen count is low, I'm cracking the window. Maybe we'll get a breeze. We'll sleep and figure it out in the morning."

"You're right." She turned so her back was to his front and switched on the book she'd been reading.

"Do you think we should continue with the plan? For the marriage?"

"Annulling the marriage?" Brielle was surprised he brought that up. She thought he was consumed with their communication problem.

"Yeah. Legally we don't qualify now."

She was quiet for a moment. "I know I deceived you, and that our marriage was mostly a business and social arrangement. I'm drug-free, but for a long, long time I never thought I would be. I thought I would die soon."

"You were in danger. It will take you some time to completely recover."

Brielle nodded. "And some of the time here has been lovely. Lila. The forest...and the sex. Didn't expect that. Had got out of the habit of looking forward to anything. So much of the time I was trying to figure out when to take a dose so I wouldn't appear intoxicated, but also not be so close to a crash I would act agitated. " She shifted on her side and traced his lower lip with one finger. "I knew I couldn't hide it from you once we were living together, but I didn't expect to overdose. I expected the marriage to end from the start. I figured my handlers would kill me once I was no longer useful. I'm thankful, it all turned out better than I expected. Whatever the future brings for us, whatever we choose, I am strong enough now to do what is needed. But I don't think we have to choose tonight."

"You are right, some of our time here has been stunning. It is silly to decide the future tonight. We are not out of danger here. That's enough to be worried about." He sounded drowsy.

"I know. With the drug... I was often made to wait, in pain, that ugly craving nothing could satisfy. Just being free of that makes me happy."

"What about the future? What do you want?"

"Karvar, I have a future now, one I can plan. I know I may not be free of health issues. Might never have a child. I tire easily, but have hopes that will improve. I quit having fairytale dreams a long time ago. Just being free is enough."

Karvar fell asleep before she did. The trillers returned from their feeding and settled on her hair. He was asleep, lying on his back He had the front of his coveralls opened, showing bare chest with a dark hair. Silky hair, she already knew.

She had not been entirely truthful with him. She wanted more than just being free of the drug, to have a measure of wellness. Deep inside, she wanted him to be her husband. But that was a fairy tale, not reality.

He'd never know. She scooted closer to him so her head was right under the small window, relishing the cool breeze. She slept, cuddled next to him.

Her armcom told her it was not yet sunrise. There was no reason for her to get up this early and the thought of lying back down next to Karvar was too tempting. She quietly used the hygenie and then slid back onto the narrow bed. In her pretend sleep, she rolled over to the side and slid an arm across him, finding the crisp soft chest hair under her forearm oddly stimulating.

They would part, politely, with respect... she would move on from New Prague, perhaps to Chen Chen, perhaps opening a small herbal plant shop. Karvar would remain on New Prague, likely as assistant to Kyler the Protectorate. Or maybe he would eventually head the Puregen Procreation Lab like his father once did.

Moisture pooled behind her closed eyelids. She was in love with him. In the early morning with the sounds of bird calls, insect trills, the soft, even breathing of the man she rested against. She might as well be honest.

Chen Chen would be best. Safer than Terra, in case she still was a target. She would move, get settled. Would she marry? That didn't seem likely, lying here with her arm over Karvar's body, as close to an embrace as she dared. She probably couldn't have children anyway. But she could adopt, or commission a Puregen Lab for a child from a surrogate. She would not live wrapped up in grief over the life she might have had...she would move on.

One of the trillers crooned softly into her hair and she drifted back to sleep.

A heavy weight rolled onto her. She struggled to open her eyes. Warm lips nibbled up and down her neck as she blinked in the early morning sunshine.

"Morning," Karvar said in a husky voice. With a few tugs her suit was down around her feet. She kicked it off and reached for Karvar, who was also getting naked. "You are very tempting in the morning."

He kissed her, a deep kiss that woke her completely. She urged him over her, on top of her. "Skin feels good," she whispered, threading her hands through his hair. Would she ever get enough of his bare flesh against hers? His nude body pressed over her from breast to tangled legs. She revelled in the silken smoothness, the heat of his skin, punctuated by patches of rough hair. A tactile feast, with her hands in his thick hair.

"Am I too heavy?"

"No, I like the feel of you." She wrapped her legs around his hips so he would really know she wanted him there, over her. "Nothing between us." They kissed, long, slow tongue kisses. His mouth moved down to her breasts, doing all the things she loved.

His hands slid from her breast to under her, then up, cupping her shoulders from beneath. She felt engulfed by him, safe, tender, like being held as a child. Except his rock hard cock was between her legs sliding over her clit. Then he was at her entrance, teasing her.

His hands gripped her shoulders tightly from beneath and as he thrust into her he pulled her slightly downward, creating even more pressure between her legs.

"Yes," His thick length went deep into her, hitting pleasure zones all along the way and the pressure of their pelvis pressed so tight gave her clit a satisfying rub.

Karvar found a rhythm that took her breath away, again and again. She flung her head back and he kissed and nibbled her neck as he continued a measured thrusting into her, pulling her whole torso downward so she met his deepest stroke with more and more pressure. It was overwhelming, entrancing. Her breathing became harsh and she lost the ability to think, only feel Karvar, *this*, again, again.

She wound tighter, knowing when she came it would be ...hard, intense, perfect. Perfect because of Karvar. She screamed as the intensive explosion consumed her, filled with the sensation of heat, slick, thick cock, clutching him tightly, barely registering that he was gasping loud himself, pounding harder and faster into her until he cried out and fell limp on her. He rolled a little to her side.

"It is my imagination, or was that..." He looked at her as though he couldn't think well enough to find the word he wanted.

Brielle smiled, a tired curve of lips. Her breath was still fast. "Yes. Whatever you meant, yes."

"Hmm."

He rolled onto his back and she slid half over him, her head on his chest. He patted her bottom with one large hand. "I think we need to try that again."

She giggled. "No objection from me."

WHEN SHE WOKE AGAIN, Karvar was in one of the pop-ups, with hot tea and meal bars. She grinned when she saw he'd copied her attire by cutting the sleeves and legs short on his coverall.

He grinned. "Like the new fashion?"

"I do. Much more comfortable, isn't it?"

"Yes.

He brought up a large holo, showing the Big Poison continent.

"Am trying to think what our next best move is."

He tapped the key pad and several lights glowed on the holo. She recognized one, the location of the Big Poison Station in the North East section of the continent that they escaped.

"So that was Glim Falls." She pointed to a light south and east of their original location.

"Yes. Here is our current location." He pointed to a light even more eastward, in the center of the continent. "To get to the Recondin Field, where the science teams are, makes the most sense. Some of Kyler's kids are there, they have stable communications. But there are only three mountain passes, and I suspect those are watched."

The holo showed the three passes. The only way around them meant an overwater route, and there were coastal mountain ranges, also.

"The flitter won't go over the mountains, it would be too dangerous to try. If we got caught in a storm and couldn't replenish our solar cells, we would freeze to death."

"Wouldn't it take a long time to fly down there anyway?"

He nodded. "Yes, the flitter was never made for speed or for long distances. Our big advantage is the continent is huge, and unless we go to a location they are expecting us to visit, it would be impossible to find us with one ship and a handful of drones. As long as we stay out here, finding us would be a rare happenstance."

Brielle thought about that. "I would rather not take risks. We have meal bars for a week or so."

"Yes. We need to start working on native foods. We could net some of those jumpers."

"Plus, Kyler probably knows by now we are in trouble."

"I think so. It is just a matter of communication." Karvar shook his head. "You know, it wouldn't be difficult to have this whole continent on the same com system as the New Prague City. It is not that we can't do it. Kyler says we need to stop being so New Prague Dome specific and start thinking about the entire planet. In this case, it would have dropped our risk level so much."

"I have often thought it was a pity New Prague didn't open this continent to immigration. It is not horribly poisonous. The Pollen Plague of a century ago was a fluke, caused by a five hundred year weather pattern. Even we have seen that most of the day here in the rainforest, the air is safe," Brielle said.

"Kyler and I will have a long talk about New Prague's communications systems when we get back. And perhaps about a southern colony, too."

Brielle opened up a holo screen on her armcom. "I'll start looking through the edible plant files. Perhaps this afternoon we can attempt to locate a few new ones. Are we safe staying here, or do you think we should move?"

Karvar sighed. "As far as safe, well, we are not safe, stranded out here. But I don't think we are easy to find. That last drone found us because I was trying to get a com connection. No doubt we are the only ones on the north side of this continent trying to connect to the com links..."

Later that day Karvar said, "Let's try some foraging. I'll forage, you hold the laser. Like we did with the salp."

Brielle made a face. "Look how that turned out. But all right.."

They traveled through the forest at a slow speed until they spotted plantains. Brielle opened her window as Karvar hovered the flitter and used the cutter to slice a bunch from the tree.

They found a giant fern with new growth. "The new growth is tender enough to eat uncooked," Brielle said. There was no good landing place, though. Karvar hovered a foot above the ground and Brielle hung half out her window to harvest the fern.

"I could find a landing place. Could use that net on some jumpers."

"I don't know. Sounds too risky. I know we have to have food, but down on the floor, even in daylight, there are predators. I am pretty sure I am not a great shooter. Maybe we should stick to things we can harvest from the window."

"Maybe."

"Perhaps we can set up some nets. I'll research it."

They returned to the base. Karvar dragged out the drone. "I'll work on the hand helds."

Chapter Six

THE NEXT FEW DAYS WERE calm to the point of boredom, except for making love whenever they wanted. Karvar dragged the drone into one of the work tents, intent on finishing the hand held lasers. They moved camp every day, and found a few new fruits to add to their diet that could be gathered from a window.

Brielle spent a great deal of time reading station files. "Karvar!"

He looked up from his table of mechanical parts.

She gestured to her holo. "Look at this!"

She enlarged the hologram screen and he looked at it.

"Fishing boats. Northwest of here is a huge fishing ground. I've eaten Prague Snapper lots of times, that's where they are caught!"

" 'Fleets of fishing boats communicate with each other via old technology radio waves, alerting their boats to locations of fish schools and trying to avoid letting competitors know the locations.' Karvar, you can make a radio. Even I can, I had to make one in science class when I was a kid."

Karvar read through the information and then looked at her. She could see the excitement in his eye. Finally, they had something they could do to try and get out of this mess.

"I'm going to look at the flitter com, it might have a radio function. We might not have to make anything." He grabbed her by the forearms and pressed a hard, warm kiss on her lips. Then he rushed out of the tent to the flitter.

Karvar found the radio function on the flitter and they listened as he switched channels, but didn't find anything. "Let's pack up camp and head northwest toward the coast. We can be on the coast in three days."

Brielle agreed and they packed up the camp.

ON THE NIGHT DESIGNATED as the next communication connection, they were almost to the northwest coast. Karvar sent the message and they waited for a reply. There was a blip on the screen, and then nothing.

Brielle yelped. "Wait. I have a file on the flitter com."

"The connection was too short to be traced, but I think we'll leave here anyway. Just in case." He set the flitter off at top speed.

They traveled for three hours and instead of launching the base, Karvar anchored them below the treetops to tree trunks, which made the flitter less balanced but fine for sleeping. Brielle made the bed and let the trillers out. The pollen count was higher here so she closed the window and turned on the air filters.

Karvar searched the new file. "It's military encryption... but not my family's secret encryption." He frowned.

"We know they have a military ship."

Karvar looked up. "No, we don't really. We know they have an older ship and drones manufactured on New Prague, though. The drone we have had its military insignia removed."

Brielle shivered. "I'm not sure that makes me feel any better. If they are in the military would it be easy to get the encryption code?"

"It would be very difficult. I think I am safe to open it."

"Wait! Don't open it yet."

"Why? It is top command encryption." He left the recliner and moved to the back bed and sat next to Brielle.

By tipping her head back Brielle could see the two moons in the night sky, far apart now, but she could see through a break in the trees.

"Karvar, what if somehow Kyler doesn't know about the bombing? What if somehow they are covering it up? Faking messages from us?" She felt him tense against her side. She sighed. "What if it is my father? He is top command."

"Your father? You think your father tried to kill you?"

Brielle couldn't look at him. Her suspicions were awful, yet they seemed to fit.

"My father isn't like yours. Your father—wasn't he always involved in your life, even when you were a child? Didn't he take you places, play with you? Things like that."

"Yes, sure. My mom might have been the Protectorate, but other than that we were a pretty ordinary family. Dad taught me how to fly a flitter. When I was little he taught me how to ride a two-wheeled bike when we were on vacation on Chen Chen. We used to play a lot of scooter polo when I was a boy, the whole family. Dad would check the schedule on the palace landing pad for times when it would be open for a couple hours."

"I never went on vacation with my father, or ever played a game with him. I went to camps as a girl, by myself. At fourteen I went to boarding school on Terra. Most years I did visit New Prague during school vacation, but not every year. Father chose my school schedule, arranged for tutors, stuff like that. He even chose my roommates, claiming security issues. All my belongings were purchased for me and I had to request things other girls had spending money to buy. I had no freedom, even though I was far away on Terra. I used to do term papers for others to make cash for secret purchases."

"Well, that is different, but that is not the same as a father trying to murder his daughter."

Brielle was silent for a while. "I think maybe he is the one who had me drugged. Absolute control, no chance of me taking my degree and getting a job somewhere, being independent. I made daily logs of my activities, for security, so his people always knew where I was. I rarely got to do things like just go shopping for an afternoon alone. I always had the roommates, and of course I spent time with their families when I wasn't in school."

Brielle turned on her side so her back was to him. Karvar had a suspicion she didn't want him to see her tears, but her voice had that husky quality that came with crying. He considered her words. Top security clearance, part of the social group closest to the Protectorate's family...

"Stars I have been so stupid!" He sat up and squeezed her shoulder. "That does make sense. Because I really think Kyler would have had half a Tier down here looking for us, if he thought something was wrong. I know he would have search parties out. And as thick as this jungle is, I don't think it would conceal us for long if he was really looking for us."

"Every time they found us, we either contacted them or did something predictable, like going to the old station," Brielle said.

"Right."

"So whoever is looking for us isn't all that powerful. They have some military weapons, though. But Kyler could send a hundred drones through this jungle. A thousand. And search parties of two-man fliers. Like they do when an aircraft goes down in the jungle or at sea."

"Yes," Karvar patted her thigh, in part because he was thankful she was able to think clearly, while he'd been in some kind of state of shock since the dome was bombed.

"I think I should delete this file. Do you agree?" He asked

"Yes. We'll figure something out."

Karvar deleted it, shut down, and got back into bed.

Lying next to her he could hear her breathe. She reached up and opened the small window, checked the pollen count on her com. Her cut down suit left her arms and legs bare, and a stream of moonlight through the trees bathed her, silvery and enticing. Karvar's mouth went dry. He was aroused—not an unusual occurrence. She shoved back her thick waves and a couple trillers flew out to feed. "We can keep the window open, the pollen count is lower now." She rolled onto her side away from him. He pulled her back against him and gently stroked her hair.

"The breeze feels good," Karvar said. He was not ready to sleep. His heart was heavy knowing his wife thought her own father was trying to kill her. And her thoughts did make sense.

How devastated he would be to find out something like that, but then his father had always been kind. High standards for behavior and work ethic, but not disapproving. Never tried to use him or his other siblings for political gain. Neither had his mother, except for her odd desire to have one of her sons marry a New Prague woman from their social group. That wasn't really too odd, though. It was a common view held by wealthy Puregens of New Prague, a group his mother had been raised in. She saw her friends and colleagues arranging marriages all the time, with good results.

He sighed. Their marriage was still unsettled. He wasn't sure if they should stay together or part when this jungle adventure was over.

The sex was amazing. They got along. A few months ago that seemed like enough, but now he wondered if he'd made a mistake, leaving love out as though it wasn't important. Shouldn't Brielle be married to someone who loved her? Shouldn't he?

All his brothers had married for love. None had married Puregens. Kellac's wife even had Zh Cle' ancestry, not that his family was racist. But it was unheard of in the dome society circles.

Wasn't love the big difference between his parent's and Brielle's? He'd always known he was loved. Known his parents loved each other and his brothers. There was laughter and kindness, along with the usual squabbles of childhood. Intellectually he knew not all families loved each other, but he had never considered what it was like to live in a family without love.

It made you vulnerable.

His brother's had all found love. Their families made them crazy and delighted them at the same time, each of them would die for their wives and children.

It was a good thing they were together. Of all the people in his family, he had never faced real danger. Or risk. He went to school with older brothers watching out for him. By the time he started training for his career, he was in his father's medical world. Backstabbing and academic mess ups, sure, he'd seen those, but no danger of not succeeding. No threats of physical danger. After gaining three degrees he went to work in the Protectorate Medical Facility in the research department, which was the most advanced facility in the Alliance. He was good at this profession, but he was also surrounded by the best of everything.

Brielle hadn't married him to spy on him. She married him in hopes he and his powerful family could help her get free. And that knowledge made all the difference in how he saw her now.

Brielle's father might have drugged her in order to make her a helpless pawn. He pulled her tighter and she covered his hand at her hip with her own, Somehow he knew that she needed to be held, to feel someone cared.

"I won't let him hurt you again." He twined his fingers with hers. His eyes finally felt tired enough to close.

Chapter Seven

TY WAS BORED. THE RECONDIN station was a small complex with few activities. While they could venture outdoors, there really wasn't much to do, unless you had a burning interest in horticulture, which he didn't have. At the last minute Chip and Grania, both swamped with upcoming coursework, had decided to remain in Judith's palace, where they had access to the libraries and data banks they needed. Dessa and her girlfriend Shay were having a mini honeymoon and Tressa and Ambli had studies they could do. Ambli was also busy with a yarn project and catching up on a series of vids he had no interest in. So he followed a few of the biologists around the Recondin fields, watching them measure the gourds, analyze insects and soil.

So. Boring.

The section of the field they lived in was fenced, a physical fence with an energy field, and there was a domed pool. He joined the girls for swimming, trying to avoid watching Ambli too closely as she splashed around in one memorable bikini after another. That was the extent of activities, other than working out in the gym.

He didn't want to think too much about Ambli in bikinis. It wasn't like she was his sister. Chip and Grania had never acted like siblings. He was much closer to Chip and Grania since they had gone through school in the same class and been constant companions back in their Sanctuary days, before Skyleen married Kyler. The girls were younger and for most school years they didn't even attend the same schools. The year they lived in the Rocondin, the girls had stayed with Skyleen in their house and yard, while he, Chip and Grania had wandered far and wide.

She was cute, but she was still a university kid. He'd be back with his Tier soon, living his life.

Ty wandered back to the station and flopped onto his bed. He turned on his com and found the book he was reading. It was the third book he'd read since they arrived here. One thing about a military career, his days were scheduled with activities clear up to bedtime. When he did have leave, he filled it with travel and all manner of activity.

His message alert popped, glowing yellow. It was from Kyler.

"Ty, this is for your eyes only. We have a situation with Karvar and Brielle. They did not communicate at the designated time. We received a short report that they were well, but it did not have Anselm encryption. I sent in a team of jungle crawlers, which took longer than a flyer, but I wanted them hidden from eyes in the sky. The Big Poison Station was firebombed, but there are no human remains and some interesting items are missing—the station flitter, cases of field nutrient bars, and Brielle's meds. So we are confident the two are somewhere in the jungle, hiding. We have vid of a few drones lurking near logical destinations, but again, no wreckage or evidence of the flitter. We think they know about the drones and are simply hiding in the forest, waiting for rescue."

"Do you want me to search for them?" Ty keyed.

"No, it may not be safe. I don't want you to get shot down by drones in the forest and none of the flyers at the Recondin Fields are equipped for military activity. Instead, pick a flyer and load survival gear and food into it. You'll have to break into the storage facility because I don't want anyone to know except you. Disable the flyer—something simple, remove a start chip. That way you can quickly replace it if you need to evacuate but no one will use it and find your stored goods. Then keep an eye on the girls so you know where they are at all times. You will need to tell them privately to be ready to evacuate. Tressa, Dessa and Shay and Ambli probably are together all the time anyway. "

"They are. Watching love dramas, season after season of them. What about the staff here?"

"I'm afraid we can't trust them with the information. But they have extensive jungle survival training, and they should have survival gear stored at different locations in the forest. So if something happens, their chances of survival are much greater than yours."

Ty decided to tell Ambli first. Then they could tell the twins, and last of all, Shay.

He found Ambli by the pool. Dessa, Tressa and Shay were visiting an area of the Recondin fields with blossoms, with the station crew. The two station scientists that were not out in the fields were in the research lab so he and Ambli were alone.

"Got enough sun cream?" With her complexion, she burned quickly.

"Yeah."

"Not too interested in blossoms?"

She rolled her eyes. "Not interested in plants at all. I wish I was back at school."

He sat down next to her, and put his feet in the water.

"I heard from Kyler, but we can't tell the crew. Just the twins and Shay."

She sat up, interested now. Her bikini today was yellow with white edging and she filled it out way too well. Did the girl have no clothes? Ty slid into the pool to cool off.

"The station up north where Karvar and Brielle were staying got firebombed, but Kyler's team did a thorough search. They got away in the flitter, with some supplies and Brielle's medications."

"You're kidding, right? Why would someone try to kill Uncle Karvar, he barely comes out of his lab!"

"It is something to do with Brielle's situation, I think. They aren't telling us everything, that's for sure. I guess we'll find out when this threat is over. But anyway, Kyler wants me to get a flitter ready with survival gear and food, in case we need to evacuate. Just us, not the science crew."

"You think there could be a firebomb here?"

"I don't know. But I am getting a flyer stocked. I'll show you which one it is in case we're separated. We'll try to get the five of us to the flitter."

"Then what?"

He shrugged. "I don't know. But we could conceivably fly across the sea to the southern tip. There is a military installation there. Or we could hide in the forest and wait for directions from Kyler."

"I'll help you stock the flyer."

BRIELLE FLOPPED ONTO her back and looked out the window. One moon, almost full, lit up the flitter through dissipating rain clouds. Rain stirred up the pollen so the windows were closed and the air filter was running. The trillers were out drinking nectar from night blooms. So funny how they came back to the ship before sunrise. It was like they adopted her. So small and delicate, yet they survived and even thrived in this jungle that was so dangerous to her and Karvar.

This continent was close to six times the size of the northern continent of New Prague. Surely it wasn't all a deadly swamp or rainforest. The Recondin fields were natural grasslands, but they were far south, past the mountains.

She tried to close her eyes, but the thought of finding somewhere safe wouldn't leave her in peace. Finally, she sat up and pulled up a holoscreen.

Where is a safe place to be on the Northern side of Big Poison?

Brielle didn't expect the search to bring her anything so she was surprised it didn't resolve quickly. It was a com, not a god, after all.

She helped herself to a piece of fruit, careful to move without disturbing Karvar. Her com now said, "Converting cache data."

The data that needed converting would be over seventy years old. This could be interesting. She slid over to the small food cabinet and made herself a cup of tea, since they were now drinking rainwater that went through a purifier that had a hot water tap.

The search continued. The light blinked. Another data conversion. How old would that data be? She'd studied some old information at school. There was data going back five hundred years before space flight, and she knew there was information even older in research libraries.

She sipped her tea until the search resolve. The original date, before updates, was nearly 300 years ago. That would have been in the colonist phase, maybe first or second generation settlers. Before the domes.

Culver Bay Colony

Culver Bay was a small North Sea colony named after Steven Adare Culver, the pilot on the colony ship Haven, United Terran States. He successfully landed the ship on the northern continent, now named New Prague, in the general vicinity of the New Prague spaceport, on the Eastern shore of the Northern Ocean.

Twenty years after landing, New Prague was a thriving colony and small settlements began to form around the city and spaceport. Fishermen followed the schools of a large mackerel-like fish that thrived in shallow warm waters along the coast of the larger southern continent, called South Continent. Culver Bay began as a temporary camp along the shore, but the beauty and mild climate soon attracted fishermen and their families year round. Due to the prevailing winds, the pollen that causes illness rarely moved into the north coast region. The village thrived for forty years until superstorm Vegas caused extensive damages and deaths in 3225. The improvement in air to sea fishing ships made it easier to live on the northern continent and travel to the fishing locations along the northern coast. That, plus the Pollen Plague of 3237 followed by the erection of New Prague City domes, ended the practice of summer camps or villages on the Big Poison shores.

While cities have sprung up in Atlanta, the third, temperate continent and Juneo, the large northern island, settlers have not flocked to the Big Poison, deeming it too wild and dangerous for simple colonization. Culver Bay was completely abandoned by 3255 and now few landmarks exist to the naked eye.

"Karvar, Karvar wake up." Brielle patted his shoulder.

He woke, blinking, and grabbed for his focals.

"What? Drone?"

"No, no we are safe. Information! This could be important."

He blinked at her.

"I'll transfer it to your com."

Soon the holo pulled up, large enough for them both to read. She handed him her cup of tea and a portion of uneaten fruit while he read through the first report and then through a dozen or so additional references.

Karvar entered some data and pulled up a map. "All right, here we are, and here is Culver Bay, according to the coordinates in the references. It will take us two days with regular stops to charge the solar cells, but it is doable. And maybe there are shellfish or other edibles on the shore. We can research that."

Brielle gave him a little hug. "That is so great, especially since our breathers are almost out of power."

He smiled back at her, his golden amber eyes practically glowing. "This buys us a lot of time."

She smiled back at him. Brielle flung her arms around him and pulled him down to the bed. "We should celebrate."

"Yes, we should." He opened the front of her suit and nuzzled her stomach with his nose and lips, a tickling move that made her grab his shoulder and clench her stomach. "Karvar."

He chuckled. "You know, you are surprisingly fit for all the drugs you used over the years."

She shrugged. "Muscles are still muscles. I took a type of dancing that involved lots of kicks based on martial arts moves. I figured my handlers wouldn't like me taking actual martial arts, but they didn't know dance."

Karvar looked up at her, his face serious. "You are stronger than you appear. In many ways, actually."

She felt her face burn. "Thanks." She scooted down the bed so they were closer to face to face and slid her hands in his hair, reveling in the thick silk between her fingers.

He moved up her body, on top of her, resting his weight on his elbows but she wanted him closer. She wrapped her legs and arms around him, trapping him, but he didn't seem to mind. In fact his lips were parted as he drew in a deep breath. She slid a finger over his lips and he engulfed it into his mouth, tongue caressing.

"Aren't you glad I woke you up?" She asked, pushing his clothes off his shoulders.

"Oh yes."

THEY HEADED NORTHWEST toward the coast, only pausing to forage a little for fruit or to charge the power cells. The air temperature increased as they neared the coast. Brielle waved a large leaf in her face as they flew.

Karvar grinned. "You know, you could take off the top of your suit. That would be cooler."

Brielle gave him a teasing look and swatted him with her fan. "I thought you were the nice brother."

"What does that mean?"

"Oh, you know. Kyler is the important, busy one with a swarm of attendants to keep people away. I've never spoken more than ten words to him. Kellac is charming, but aloof... always looking over people's heads to find his wife. Kaistril is incapable of carrying on a civilized conversation unless he is talking about his family, or armament trade deals, which I know nothing about and care about even less."

Karvar grinned. "That does sound like my brothers."

She frowned at him. "You are the one with all the social skills. The one known for being a graceful dancer, the one who makes the old women giggle. The one invited absolutely everywhere because you will show up and be charming."

"I sound so manly. And I don't go to everything, I turn down lots of invitations."

"Oh, please. I know you have a social secretary who does that for you."

He laughed. "True. Morris plans my calendar and even sets out my clothes."

She grinned. "I knew it!"

He pouted and she giggled.

"I am still manly."

"You are," she agreed. "I'll show you how manly I think you are when we park for the night."

They traveled west for the rest of the day and settled in the late afternoon to recharge. The day was still steamy hot but clouds had rolled in. By the time the base was launched and the flitter was parked rain poured down. Laughing, Brielle pulled him out into the rain and unfastened his cut-off suit, then tossed her own into the puddle already forming on the base floor. They made love in the warm rain.

"I think I now find rain arousing," Karvar murmured into her hair later, while they rested on the bed.

Chapter Eight

BRIELLE WOKE THE NEXT morning with an ache in her chest. *Am I ill?* Everything had been going so well! They hadn't been exposed to much pollen at all, and she had worn her breather whenever counts were high, which hadn't been often, or stayed inside the flitter with the air system running.

She went to see Karvar at his work table. "Good Morning," Karvar smiled at her, his eyes behind his viewer were soft.

"Morning," she croaked. She cleared her throat. "I think I am sick."

Karvar placed a hand on her forehead and then went back to the container of med supplies. He checked her over and gave her an injection. "That should lower the fever. We need to keep your fluids up in this heat."

She nodded, too discouraged to say anything. She wanted to cry, but she didn't want Karvar to see her tears. She was so...angry. Scared. Betrayed once again by her body. Of course, her body would betray her now, right when she and Karvar were coming to some kind of understanding about their marriage.

Brielle got sicker, dizzy and exhausted, as the day grew. She knew they traveled west. She dutifully drank the liquids Karvar gave her, she let him help her to the hygenie since standing made her wobble.

KARVAR FLEW WEST UNTIL he had to stop to charge the ship. Perhaps he should consider the contact file. They had deleted it, but with some work he could pull it back up. Of course, he couldn't fly and work on the com at the same time...

But the coast would be best. Good air...Maybe their coms had not recorded pollen levels correctly. Or maybe Brielle had something other than Pollen Plague. Without a medlab he was hampered.

And Brielle was in grave danger. She was still recovering, still needed a long nap every day, was still taking medications to help regulate her heart. He worried their food supply wasn't giving her the nutrients she needed to recover properly.

The night passed with no improvement in Brielle's condition. She had started coughing so he used containment protocols, though it was probably too late if she had something he could catch.

"Karvar," she said after he crawled into bed with her. "Promise you'll watch out for my little sisters. I think it might be my father. Must be him."

"God, Brielle. Of course, I'll watch out for your sisters. But I won't have to because you'll be there doing it. This is just temporary."

"Maybe. But maybe it is the natural end to a life damaged by years of drug abuse."

She coughed a long, painful spasm. Later, when she'd had a sip of water and calmed a little she said. "I am certain it is my father, Karvar. No proof, though, just my gut feeling."

"Of course I will help your sisters. I don't want you to worry about them, Brielle. Sleep now. Think about getting well."

She might not make it. Karvar faced the harsh truth. Her body, especially her heart, had taken years of abuse. If they were at the palace, she would have so much available, even artificial hearts to sustain life until a suitable organ could be cloned. But out here...

He'd get her to the beach. There would be a cooling breeze. The sound of the sea would be soothing.

Late the next day Brielle slept behind him on the bench bed. Her breathing was raspy. As soon as they landed, he would scrounge up something for a steam tent. They were within twenty miles of the coast, he would go another half hour and launch the base, set up camp. When they were settled, he would tell her. He wasn't going to end the marriage because of her past addiction. He would end it if she desired, but he hoped she would remain his wife. They would approach their marriage, as did others, working things out as they came up...

Did he love her? Was this love? Mostly he was scared to death she would die. But he wanted her to be happy, wanted to be with her, and not just for sex.

The trillers shot out of Brielle's hair, fluttering wildly, cries loud and piercing. *Drone!* Karvar dived into the deep forest greenery and Brielle woke with a hoarse scream.

"Trillers alerting...drone!" It took all his concentration to keep the flitter from crashing into trees. "Try to harness up."

He couldn't look to see if she was getting harnessed. He still had no sight on the drone.

Something huge flew in front of the flitter and they halted abruptly, springing backward and then slowly crashing to the forest floor. Karvar stared at the screen in shock. A net, they'd flown into a net! He unharnessed and went back to Brielle, holding the laser.

"We're caught. I'm sorry, Brielle. They had some type of net." He stroked her hair back as another spasm of coughing wrenched her whole body.

The door of the flitter flew open.

"Drone! Stop the drone." Karvar screamed at the man who peered into the flitter. The man jumped back and looked at the treetops.

"Drones," he yelled and Karvar saw several more people come out of the undergrowth.

Karvar stared at the man in confusion. He was not a New Prague Protectorate Guard, instead of a uniform he wore tanned reptile hide, like the hide of some of the jungle Fringed Lizards. He held an old-fashioned projectile weapon in his hand. His hair was slicked back and worn in a knot at the back with a tie covered in small seashells. Brown and green scales ran down his outer arms, but his chest and inner arms were free of scales.

Zh Cle'. The whole group was Zh Cle'. He'd known for years there were mixed Zh Cle'-human colonists on New Prague, living quietly, working in the shipbuilding factories. But he'd had no idea there were weaponized groups of them in the jungle. He bet Kyler didn't know either.

A glint of silver caught in his peripheral vision.

"Drone!" He yelled, just as one of the group yelled, "Ten o' clock".

The group trained their weapons and Karvar dragged Brielle down to the floor of the flitter, covering her. There was no time to drag her out of the vehicle.

Sharp, ear piercing cracks pounded through his head, the screech and tear of metal. Brielle screamed. A hard thud rocked the flitter and pieces of the thin debris rained down on them. Glass shattered, raining on him, small, sharp cuts, but he was glad Brielle was under him, safe from the flying debris.

Then it was over. He could smell burnt electronics. Two men yanked open the side door of the flitter and helped him out.

"Help my wife. She is very ill."

A couple of the Zh Cle' helped her out of the dented flitter.

Brielle continued to cough. Karvar dropped his stunner.

"I'm Karvar Anselm, my wife Brielle. We were at the Big Poison Science station, but it was fired on," Karvar said.

The long-haired man lowered his weapon. "I'm Ernie Houlihan. You flew into one of our boundary nets."

He looked over his shoulder. "It's all right. Couple of scientists. The lady is real sick." Eight men and women, athletic and dressed in reptile skin like Ernie, lowered their metal weapons.

"She's ill, Pollen Plague, I think. Our breathers died four days ago."

As he said that he noticed that none of the Zh Cle' wore breathers.

"We can help."

Karvar carried Brielle, first on a dirt trail and then on a sanded path. The path ended at a small clearing, surrounded by small wooden huts raised on stilts or built into large trees. In the center was a garden area, grown on vertical walls, surrounding a pool. A small community area with tables and benches and a fire pit were in the clearing, also. All the houses had staircases built with rope, probably meant to be drawn up by the home dweller. Several small, squat lizards rooted around the perimeter. A wide path left the village and in the distance, Karvar could see a sandy shore and the sea.

"Welcome to Culver Bay."

An hour later Karvar sat in a small hut with Brielle. An elderly Zh Cle' woman, Mrs. Breen, was waving a small clay pot with a spout of steam around Brielle's nose and mouth. "Here you go. This will steam for about fifteen minutes, and we will repeat every hour. It will help her breathing."

Karvar nodded and took the clay steamer. "You don't have a way to check her oxygen levels?"

"Not here, son. But we have radioed one of the ships to head this way."

"Ships?"

"Scampers. We are a fishing village. There are rich waters here, full of scamp."

Scamp, a mild flavored, shrimp-like seafood. He'd eaten it thousands of times. "So you have contact with the Northern Continent?"

"Yes, we sell in the coastal markets, normally at Port Harold."

"Brielle is weak, she is recovering from a long illness. I would like to transport her to New Prague as soon as possible."

"We will do all we can to help her. Our healers have dealt with the Pollen cough many times. You will see, she will be all right. But you must talk to Ernie now. The drone concerns us."

Brielle, settled into a narrow bed, opened her eyes. "Go, Karvar. I already feel better."

"I'll be back as soon as I can."

Karvar spent the next hour with the Zh Cle' men and women of Culver Bay Security. They sat in the open area of the clearing at the tables near the pool. Small children played in the water while older children were brought back from the beach until the drone threat was over.

"So is this a fishing camp, or do you live here year-round?"

"A few live here year round, but during monsoon season this all turns into a giant mud puddle. Dangerous with just these wooden huts. Many go back to the dome and take temporary jobs, others move to other compounds in the mountains and work in the mines or other jobs."

"How many villages are there?"

"Seven or so. Also some big fruit plantations which are practically villages in themselves. So most of us spend about four months away from here."

"I'm a bit astonished. We didn't know anyone was settled here."

"We are off the regular power grid. Most of us use solar power. We communicate by radio, but New Prague doesn't monitor radio waves. Communication in the domes is through satellite receivers, you know."

Karvar nodded. He knew.

"Are you Karvar Anselm, son of the Protectorate Judith?" A young woman asked this.

"Yes, I am."

"Will you attempt to remove our villages and camps?" An older woman asked.

"No. Of course not. I'm just astounded you are here." He paused for a moment. "I can get protections set up for your camps and villages. Kyler is not opposed to Zh Cle' citizens. In fact, one of my sister-in-laws is part Zh Cle'. But how do you stay healthy here?"

"Ahh, well, the move into domes in the past was not completely motivated by truth. There was big money involved in the dome contract, " Ernie said. "It took less than a decade to develop an effective treatment for Pollen Plague, and people of Zh Cle' ancestry are less affected by it. So when Zh Cle' fishermen started camping here they noticed what a fine place it was to live, for half the year at least."

"We use the breathing treatments your wife is having if we have been in the jungle. Small children and our elders take them daily. They are made from a plant we cultivate."

Karvar noticed the vertical garden walls were thick with greenery.

"The drones are after us. They are some faction, not New Prague Protectorate Guard, Older drone models. We are not certain Kyler knows we are in distress. And I'm not sure how many drones there are. We have never seen a large group of them."

Karvar showed them the hologram of the continent with the places they had seen the drones. "I have pieces of one that got swallowed by a mud salp."

The villagers looked at him and he related the story of the salp vomiting out the drone, much to their amusement.

"It sounds like their drones may be affected by the satellite communication issue just as your flitter is. We will send radio communications to all the villages in the forest."

"Do you have any contact with the scientists in the far south? I have young relatives at the Recondin Field Station. Do you have any way to get a message there?"

"No. We have heard about the Recondin Fields, but have rarely traveled that far south, though there is some good hunting on the plains. I don't know of anyone living down there."

"We thought about traveling there, but the passes might be guarded by drones. I know they have nearly constant satellite communication with New Prague City."

Ernie looked at him for a moment. "Julio, get up to the radio tower and send an alert about the drones. You paid attention to the locations?"

Julio, a young man with dark hair and eyes, nodded, holding up a piece of thick paper.

"Good man. Get the alert out now, and tell them to stay tuned for further developments. I'd like to get scouts out. I suspect a ship is hiding at some base in the forest, a base for directing the drones. Flying down here from the domes so often could be noticed."

Karvar hadn't thought of that, but it made sense.

"I'll get up to the tower myself in an hour. Tell the elders. I'd like to get hunting parties out looking for this ship."

They helped Karvar get Brielle's medication out of the flitter and set up a guard around the village. Karvar joined Brielle, who was already breathing better. He stayed with her, consenting to a breathing treatment of his own and an early night in the small clinic. Brielle was sleeping deeply, and her temperature was lower. A type of intravenous tubing was boosting her fluid level, and a steamy breathy treatment was placed near her face every hour, to remove the pollen from her lungs. He questioned the healer about everything, impressed with the care Brielle was given despite the primitive conditions. They did use solar power and had small receptors high up in the canopy which fueled necessary equipment. He flopped down onto the small cot on the other side of the room and fell asleep.

The next morning Ernie met Karvar in the community area in the village center. "I was talking to one of my men last night, about the Recondin Fields. We do know of a very narrow pass discovered in just the last decade. We call it Hidden Pass."

Karvar nodded. "I doubt my flitter could make the journey now. It needs major repairs."

Ernie. "Well, we have the bladder craft."

"The what?"

"Local flying machine. One of the local sea plants has a bladder that rises to the surface. We harvest those and use them for a propeller craft. Maybe you and a couple of the guards could head down to the Recondin fields in one of those."

The idea astonished him. "How long would it take?"

Ernie shrugged. "Not sure. Day down, day back?"

A day. He could contact Kyler tomorrow! "Let me see the aircraft."

Chapter Nine

"BRIELLE, BRIELLE."

She struggled with her heavy eyelids. Karvar was standing over her.

"What are you wearing?" He wasn't in the cut up coveralls, instead, he was in a jacket and pants made of dark green leather of some sort, textured.

"Oh. The Zh Cle' settlers here make clothing out of local lizards. They loaned me the clothes. I'm going with them, down to the Recondin station to get Kyler's kids out of there."

"You're leaving here? What about the drones?" She struggled to sit up, and he helped her.

"While you were sleeping the past two days, scouts determined the approximate location of the base they are coming from, in the wide central pass down to the Recondin Station."

She nodded and was quiet for a moment, gauging how well she felt. She made a fist and noted she wasn't as weak as yesterday, but she didn't feel normal, either. She couldn't ask him to take her with them, she was already too much of a burden.

"How long do you think you'll be away?"

"I think a day down and a day back. The villagers can travel through the forest in small float crafts they make. I guess they do it all the time for hunting."

"I see. It's good to be undercover in the trees in case they send out more drones."

Karvar sat down next to her on the bed and took her hand. "I don't like leaving you alone, but you are doing very well with their medical treatments. I think this is a safe place. Pollen levels here are nearly nonexistent. And you are so much better."

"I am better. The healers here are all very kind to me."

"One of the reasons I'm going down is that I know Kyler can communicate with his kids. We can end this in a couple days, as soon as I see Ty and the rest. I think that is best, rather than wait for you to be well."

"I understand. When do you leave?"

"Within the hour. I told them I would leave as soon as I could talk to you. I didn't want you to feel deserted."

She blinked back tears, hoping he didn't notice. "I will be fine. I can stay here and regain my strength and you can get in touch with Kyler. This is the best plan."

A crushing sadness surrounded her heart. This was the end of their tiny seedling of a marriage. The days before she fell sick, she'd had such hopes— secret, foolish hopes. But in a few days the Protectorate would be here and their time alone together would be over. She took a steadying breath. "Have a safe journey, Karvar. I'm glad we met the villagers and they can help keep Kyler's kids safe."

Karvar bent over, gave her a gentle hug and brushed a kiss across her forehead. Her forehead, like she was an elderly aunt! "You'll feel much better by the time I get back."

She didn't want him to see her cry. She scooted down on her pillows, eyes closed tight so tears wouldn't seep down her cheeks.

"Yes, I'm sure I will."

He left.

Brielle cried herself to sleep. She knew all along that this marriage would end... she'd built up foolish hopes from a few passionate moments. I forgot Karvar's had lots of passionate moments, with lots of women. My lack of... of a Life is why I'm so vulnerable.

When she woke a young woman sat with her, red-haired with golden skin showing a faint marking of scales on her arms. The woman held a tablet, a large one like those used in a library.

"What are you reading?"

The girl looked up. She had a round face and big round eyes, warm hazel. She smiled and placed the tablet on a small counter. "Hello. I'm Nancy. I was studying for an anatomy test while you slept."

"Oh, there's a college down here?"

"Well, no. But there is the Universal Healer's Course materials, through the Alliance Library system. Many schools use the same texts, but really anyone can access them. I can upload my exams to the Medical Board once a month through the Library, too. But next year I will have to go to school in the dome, because I'll need labs and practicals."

She bustled around the room and brought Brielle a mug of savory broth. "I'll give you a breathing treatment soon, but you probably need something nutritious."

"Did Karvar and the rescue party get off all right?"

"Yes. My fiancé Effan is with the group. He does a great deal of hunting so is experienced flying in the deep woods."

Nancy wore a healer's smock, but below her knees Brielle could see she was wearing leggings made of the lizard hide.

"Isn't that hide your pants are made of hot to wear? It is not cool here."

Nancy smiled as she prepared the breathing treatment. "Here, feel it. It breathes."

Brielle pinched some of the leather and found it was more like fabric. It had a smooth texture and was barely heavier than silk used for gowns. "That is remarkable."

"And impenetrable by crawlers."

"What are those?"

"Insects from the soil. If you have skin contact they can burrow into your skin. Painful! So we wear boots and leggings of fringed lizard hide."

"Is that why you live in houses on poles?"

"That and the monsoons. Come rainy season we slosh through a foot of muddy water. Most people go back to New Prague City."

Brielle felt almost normal the next morning. It was such a relief and her heart lightened. So much of what she wanted in life required her to be well. Or at least not bedridden!

"Do you think I could get out of this room? Maybe a walk down to the beach?"

Nancy looked at the data she'd just entered. "I think so. Let me go talk to the healer."

She returned a few moments later. "They think it would be fine to walk down to the beach. Let me get you some clothes and then we can go."

Brielle changed into the silken lizard skin shirt and pants, simple pull-ons with adjustable waists, that Nancy gave her. She had socks of the same material and boots made of a thicker hide. She also handed her a lizard skin jacket that could be fastened around the neck to hang in back like a cape if not needed.

"The jacket is just in case, like if we had an accident while walking and had to stay in the forest for some time. We won't need it, but it is a simple safety custom we all follow."

That explained all the men they had met when they first arrived wearing capes. She'd thought it was pretty exotic.

The path to the beach went through thick woods, but occasionally she caught a glimpse of a jungle house, raised on poles or built onto a tree trunk. The path had been cobbled at one point and was broad enough for four people to walk abreast. Smaller paths and trails branched off it, some dirt and mud, others covered with sand.

The path ended at a wide swath of beach bordered on one end by a couple of long docks. Most of the wooden docks were empty of boats since t but here and there a small boat floated, tied to the docks.

"The fishing fleet is out so the docks are pretty empty today."

Children played everywhere, in the water, in the sand, while a few adults watched over them. Brielle and Nancy joined a small group of adults sitting under a large umbrella.

"I see the children are in bathing suits. I guess you don't have to worry about safety on the beach?"

"Near the village, the predators have been eliminated and few come out in the bright light of day. We do have to caution children from straying away from the main beach. It is always a concern with the older children, wanting to find a place away from adults."

"Yes, I see that would be a concern. How do you handle it?"

"All of our able-bodied rotate on a patrol group, which check all the likely places. Most of us spent our summers here so we actually know the best places all ready."

"Do any of you live here year-round?"Brielle asked,

"We do," a woman in her thirties holding an infant spoke. "But when our children are older we will go up north to Port Harold. There are schools there for older children that offer more than we could do here. I'm Lil, by the way."

"It would be lovely to have a real school here, so we didn't have to take our older children north."

"You can't have a school here?"

"Well, funding a real school with labs and equipment is expensive. So are teacher's salaries. We homeschool using the Alliance library courses. Older kids go to Upper school in Port Harold so it is easier for them to enter the University if they want."

Brielle nodded. "I see. Up in New Prague City people don't even know there is a village here." She paused, wondering if she should speak. "Karvar...you know my husband is the youngest son of Judith the Past Protectorate, brother to Kyler? We could talk to him and see if they could help."

The women looked at each other and Brielle wondered if she had said something wrong.

"We are afraid of a homestead act that would cost us our lands," Lil said. "We are fishers, but in the forest are small farmers who have worked hard to develop farmland, and a few tiny settlements. It would be awful if they lost their homes."

"It has happened before," said a younger woman. "Especially to Zh Cle' settlers."

"We would need to grandfather all of the current residents before any new could come. And I would hope we could protect this land. The north is all cities and industry...they are talking about changes so people have more access to green areas, but with the war that hasn't been a priority."

Brielle paused. Was it common knowledge? But these people needed to know the Protectorate was not racist. "Do you know that one of the Anselm brothers is married to a woman of Zh Cle' Ancestry?"

"No! Which one?" All the women stared at her with avid interest.

"Gema. She is married to Kellac."

"Oh, the one with the twins! How exciting." The information brought broad smiles to the group of parents.

It was a pleasant afternoon. After chatting for a while, Brielle waded for a bit in the ocean, wishing she had a bathing suit. She dozed for a short time while Nancy went to get some lunch to share under the umbrella. Then she and Nancy left before she got too tired. Her trillers had flown into the woods while she chatted on the beach. It seemed several families kept them as pets.

"If you have quite a group of them in your house, it often keeps the pollen count down during wind shifts. Usually, our wind comes from the sea, but once a year or so we'll get a forest wind."

The trillers joined her as they walked slowly back to the village.

A thought suddenly occurred to her. "Nancy, you use the library in New Prague? The big one? And upload and download texts?"

"Yes, the New Prague City library is part of the Alliance Library system. I often get digital texts from them."

"But, how do you communicate with them from here? You are not on the satellite com system."

"Oh! We use radio. All Alliance Libraries can communicate by radio, send files and data. It is part of the Library System All Worlds Education Initiative. Even colony worlds and Zh Cle' worlds have access to knowledge." She paused. "It was a huge deal for our Zh Cle' families who lived on Reservation worlds, so we learned all about it in history. Our history."

Brielle stopped dead in the pathway. She'd learned that in school, too. "So you have a radio that communicates to the library."

"Sure. It's in the school."

"Can you take me there? I have a plan."

"I can, but we'll need to take a flyer," Nancy said. "The little kids go to school in the village, but the older kid fly up on the ridge. That's where the radio tower is."

Back in the village, Nancy talked to the head healer and then Brielle followed Nancy to her home, a small hut built into a tree.

"I just told her you were curious about our flyers and we would go up to the ridge for the view. She said to make you wear a breather."

She followed Nancy into the hut, amazed at all the colorful wall hangings and curtains, the woven vine furniture with deep cushions. "This is just gorgeous."

Nancy grinned. "My mother. She sews, knits. All of it. And water soaked vines can be twisted and formed into furniture. It is quite a skill to learn."

The flyer was out on a balcony in a small shed. "We call it the terrace. Don't ask me why."

The flyer had two seats attached to a frame that held some type of bladder that made it float, and with a propeller for direction.

"What it this thing?" Brielle tapped the balloon and it made a drum sound.

"There are these kelp plants, we call them kelpies. Big, ugly things. They float in beds where fish feed. We hunt for the bladders. As long as they don't get punctured, the gas remains. The rind is really tough."

"What powers it?"

"Solar cells."

Brielle donned her breather and sat in the small seat. Nancy handed her a headset to cover her ears. "They are noisy!"

Nancy started the engine and pushed off manually from the back door of the shed. Soon they were bussing above the forest. "Twenty minutes."

The ridge was an enormous stone cliff rising above the forest. They came to a large rectangular building with a terrace all around. A tall metal tower stood at one end. No one was there.

"I'm surprised it is empty."

"Normally someone is here, but since your husband flew south they must have decided to leave it. It will be fine."

The door had a keypad and Nancy typed into it.

Inside was one large room with tables and desks. Data cabinets lined one wall.

"What do you want to do? Look something up?"

"No, I wanted to try and communicate with a librarian. Kyler, Karvar's brother has all those university kids. Two of them stayed in New Prague instead of going to the Recondin Station. They needed access to the library for their class work. They should be there at the library. Wait, what time is it in New Prague City?"

"They are two hours behind us."

Brielle grinned. "So they should be there, researching away. If I can radio a message to the kids, Grania and Chip Chip Nur."

Nancy showed her the microphone. "Make your message and I'll send it. Best to write it down first."

"Alliance Librarian,

"This is Brielle Anselm, wife of Karvar Anselm, sister-in-law to Kyler the Protectorate. We currently have lost communication and had to leave the Big Poison Science Station. It was damaged." She paused. Damaged a lot!

"We are now at the Culver Bay fishing village. They have a radio tower outside town and use the library frequently." She read the coordinates Nancy had given her. "We only have radio for communication. I would like to talk to Grania Anselm, daughter of Kyler, or his ward, Chip Chip Nur. They are probably in the library working on University projects. Can you connect me?"

"This is Pol Naolt, I received your message, Danger Ridge. I know the two individuals. If you will hold I will go see if they are here today."

"The red light will come on when they transmit." Nancy handed her a cup of sweet tea. "So Kyler adopted all those kids? The ones from the Hub that he rescued?" She grinned, sheepishly. "I was just a kid when they showed up with the Recondin and we were in New Prague city then. It was like a fairy tale!"

Brielle grinned. "I was in school on Terra but I heard about it. Kyler couldn't adopt them all. Ty has a genetic code that placed him in a family on a Puregen tech world that was invaded by the Gorvas, so he could still have family, somewhere. Some legal thing with that planet. And it is still in chaos after the invasion, so many killed or converted to cyborgs. Kyler could be his guardian but not adopt him. And Chip Chip Nur comes from a real outback world that is not in the Alliance. They don't have a centralized government. Chip preferred to keep his name and someday search that world for clues as to who his family might be. So Kyler is their guardian. But Kyler and Skyleen adopted all the girls and treat the boys like their own."

The red light flashed.

"Hello? This is Chip Chip Nur and Grania Anselm."

"Chip, Grania. This is Brielle. Karvar's wife. Our communication got messed up."

"Are you all right?"

"Yes, I am in Culver Bay. Did you get the coordinates?"

"Yes. I already contacted Kyler."

"Karvar headed south with the villagers. They are flying through a narrow pass called Hidden Pass to get down to the Recondin Station. The other passes are covered by attack drones."

"I can contact Ambli and the girls. Ty has a military com set up and I don't have access to him. But the Recondin Station can communicate here in the dome." This voice was lighter, Grania talking.

"Yes, but they are on a twenty-four hour on and off communication system. Trust me, Brielle, Kyler and Judith are kicking themselves for not getting planet-wide communication set up. It's just that so few people live outside the domes."

"I know. I think Karvar is safe but he was worried about the kids at the station."

There was a pause.

"Kyler Anselm here. How are you Brielle? "

"I'm fine. Had a touch of Pollen Plague but the village healer helped."

"Karvar is not there?"

"No, he is flying to the Recondin Station though a pass these locals know."

"Can I have those coordinates?"

"I'll check."

"I can find them," Nancy said. She went to a large cupboard and brought out an actual paper map.

"This is Nancy, a healer in training who brought me to the radio tower."

"Hi." Nancy cleared her throat. "I have the coordinates for the pass."

When she was done Kyler thanked her. "Brielle, you probably need to get some rest. Thank these good people for me. I have a Protectorate Squad in the air. Please reassure the village people we have no intention of interfering with their colony and I can afford them legal status to protect their lands."

Nancy's eyes got huge. "Gosh, we didn't even have to ask for legal status," she whispered.

"I'm signing off. I will be arriving on the southern continent is five hours or so. You take care, Brielle."

"I will. Thank you, Kyler."

Nancy sat staring at the radio.

"The Protectorate family has no issues with Zh Cle's ancestry, remember? They love Gema and the boys. Their twin boys have some Zh Cle' markings on their arms, a lot like yours." She leaned close. "Just between you and me, her boys are really a handful! But adorable."

Before they left they tried to contact Karvar but the canyons they were flying through didn't have good access. "I can set up a repeating message. They could suddenly get radio," Nancy said.

TY WAS IN HIS BEDROOM, a small cubicle with a cot, utilitarian desk and cupboards, not unlike his quarters on base. They'd had their afternoon meal, and now he was trying to think of something to do. Swim? Workout? Read a book? He pulled on his swimsuit.

There was a knock on his door and Ambli burst in.

"Hey!" He scowled at her. She could have walked in on anything.

"News! I have a communication from Kyler"

He frowned. "It is day off."

"I know, but this is radio. Through the Alliance Library. It is on radio, did you know?"

"I did know. It's part of the Alliance Treaty Information Act."

Ambli rolled her eyes. "Well, I have radio access through my com. You don't." Ty had a hi-tech military com but Ambli had a state of the art armcom that she received as a birthday gift.

"Well, no one thought we were going back in time," he said. No radio app was a design flaw on the military com, though. He would see if he could get radio access added. Especially if he was to spend any more time in the wilderness.

"Here, listen. It popped up as an alert, not a normal one, but directed me to a radio frequency."

"Ty, I'm assuming you got a ship ready." Kyler's voice came from the com. "I want you and the girls to evacuate. I have a route prepared. Since you will be in a science station flyer, quite different than Karvar's flitter, I think you can safely fly out to the coast and then north to a fishing village on the northwest shore. Save these coordinates. Brielle is at the village. We are redirecting our communication satellite, but it will take a couple of hours. Karvar is on his way to you at the station, but his flyer is not fast. It is a local built propeller flyer. We hope to either intercept him or communicate with him in the pass. I'm in flight for the southern continent. We suspect a mole is at the science station so get the girls out without mentioning this."

Ty pulled on his clothes. "We'll retrieve our baggage at a later date. Do you know where the girls are?"

She nodded. "They are watching vids in our room." All the girls shared dorm-like quarters.

"How do we do this?"

Ambli breezed by him. "They are bored out of their minds, like we are. It will be easy."

It was. Ambli popped her head in the room. "Come on. Quiet, though. Ty is going to sneak us out for a flight. It'll be fun."

Just like that they were harnessed in the flyer. Ty went to the three other fliers and quickly disabled them. That should keep the mole out of their hair. He tossed the small part he removed from each ship in a covered cupboard in the rear and got the ship in air.

The ship was quiet, engineered to allow the science crews to observe wildlife without startling them with loud noise. Ty flew away from the compound, suspecting the rest of the crew were in their rooms or in the pool area.

"So listen up, you all. We are heading to a place called Culver Bay. It is a village up the coast. Brielle and Karvar are there. This is on Kyler's order. He thinks there is a mole working with someone who is after Brielle."

"I didn't know there was a village on the Big Poison," Dessa looked confused.

"No one knew. It is a Zh Cle' fishing village."

"Zh Cle'?" Shay asked. "Since when have Zh Cle' lived on New Prague?"

The four looked at her. "Like, forever, Shay."

She shrugged. "I thought they couldn't immigrate here. DNA tests."

"The Puregen tech worlds have DNA tests in their constitutions, New Prague doesn't," Tressa said.

"Not because the Puregens here are so open-minded, but when the factories get a big order they have to pull in thousands of workers quickly. Didn't you pay attention in History of New Prague?" Ambli sounded a little snippy.

Ty grinned. There was just something about Shay that irked him. But Dessa loved her so he kept out of it.

"But what about all our belongings?" Shay asked.

"Kyler is sending a squad down. They'll retrieve all our stuff."

"But it is not packed up! We need to go back." Shay looked a little wild-eyed. Ty surreptitiously turned on a viewer so he could face forward but examine her. He shared a glance with Ambli who sat up front with him.

"We have food and water and our coms. We'll be fine. It is a six-hour flight, no biggie. We'll be there by nightfall, meet up with everyone. "

"But I have things I need!"

"What?"

She didn't answer, but sat back against the seat with a flounce of hair.

The flight along the seashore was lovely. While Shay still seemed put out, Tressa passed out meal pacs and juice bottles.

Ty got a text.

Ambli: Do you think Shay is the mole?

Ty: Maybe. What do you know about her?

Ambli: Not much. She went to school on Jupiter Dome, just moved here with her parents to work on the Homestake project.

Ty nodded. They had imported several thousand workers to build hub components for the new space hub out by Farradae.

Ty: Well, let's keep an eye on her. There is only one weapon aboard, mine. At least that I am aware of.

Ambli: She was in her undies and got dressed right in front of everyone. Doubt she is armed.

Ty: Good. But keep an eye out.

Chapter Ten

NANCY PARKED THE SMALL flyer back in her treehouse shed and the two walked slowly to the village. It was fairly late with the sun low and Brielle did not enjoy the dim walk through the forest. She was very tired, also.

"We'll be there in a couple minutes," Nancy reassured her. "And you'll go straight down for a nap. This was a great deal more activity than I had intended."

The trillers burst out from under her hair, which was pulled up into a tail. They flew around, agitated. "Oh no," Brielle whispered, grabbing Nancy's arm to stop her. "There might be a drone. The trillers get agitated around them."

Nancy pulled her off the path into the thick undergrowth. "Pull on your jacket and hood. Here in the shade, we'll blend into the woods."

They crept from tree to tree, and found a thick clump of vines to hide in.

A tremendous roaring and crashing, shouts and screaming. Nancy jumped up, but Brielle pulled her down. "Wait."

A man yelled at the villagers but they couldn't understand all his words. A cold shiver ran through Brielle. She recognized the voice. She'd been right all along. "It's my father," she whispered.

"Good, then everything is all right." Nancy rose again.

Brielle yanked her down. "No, no! Nothing is right. We are in deadly danger. He is here to kill me. I did not do what he groomed me for since I was a girl. He wanted me to spy on Karvar and his family. I think he is selling information to the Gorvas."

Nancy looked at her in horror, reminding her of Karvar and his difficulty trying to understand her relationship with her father. Brielle shrugged. "We need to hide."

"I know a place we can hide." Nancy grabbed her hand and they crept further away from the village and the sounds of the engines.

The trillers settled back underneath her ponytail. "The trillers have settled down," she whispered to Nancy. "They get excited when drones are around. So the drones must have landed or something. They must be searching the village."

"They'll go down to the beach soon. Come on." They broke through undergrowth to a dirt trail. "Can you run? I do know some hiding places where we can rest."

"I'll try."

They jogged but Brielle was soon out of breath. They hid in vines while she rested. "Where are we going?"

The trillers went crazy again, Brielle grabbed Nancy and they crawled deep into the undergrowth, disturbing a nest of jumpers that leaped out of the undergrowth with deep throated protests.

Brielle crouched, trying to breathe quietly like Nancy. Nancy tapped her arm and pointed. In the distance, they could see a small section of the beach path. Children and adults hurried up the path to the village, guards in Protectorate uniform with them.

"I should turn myself in," Brielle whispered. "It is me they want."

"But you said he'd kill you!" Nancy gripped her arm with a surprisingly strong grasp.

They were quiet, catching their breath.

"I have an idea," Nancy said.

Brielle followed her through the undergrowth. "It's slow, but I think we should stay off the paths," Nancy said.

They trudged for some time away from the village. Brielle felt sick thinking about the friendly villagers being held captive by her ruthless father.

They came to a small clearing with a tree house and a ladder built by notching the tree trunk and adding some hand holds.

"Laredo, Auggy. Are you there?"

There was some commotion and a Zh Cle' boy about Nancy's age slipped agilely down the trunk.

"What's going on? We saw the drones."

Nancy pulled her forward. "This is Brielle Anselm. Married to Karvar, brother to Kyler."

"The Protectorate Kyler?"

Brielle nodded.

"Karvar and the security team went through the Hidden Pass to rescue their nieces and nephews. Some rogue officer is trying to kill Brielle," Nancy continued while the boys stared at her.

"It's a long story."

"What's important, they are at the village. I think they are holding the village hostage."

"How many?"

"We don't know, but the flyer isn't large. Maybe eight men?"

"Armed men," Brielle said.

They all stood there for a moment silent, while the idea of armed men in the little family village sunk in.

Nancy took a breath, "Do you have the blowpipes? And the darts?"

"Yeah. We could sneak up on them."

Brielle looked at the boys. Some looked around fourteen or so, the oldest was perhaps Nancy's age.

"No."

They looked at her.

"Listen. I can't allow you to do this. These men are killers. I am just going to surrender. Otherwise, you are all in danger."

"No, we can do this," the oldest boy insisted. "Really. The poison on the darts is a special concentrate, works almost immediately."

"Almost? So they still have time to shoot?"

"Maybe, but they will be really dizzy."

Brielle frowned. "What are a bunch of kids doing with poison darts?"

One of the boys grinned. "School science project. A long time ago a student did some research on Terran rainforests, where some tribes used a fast-acting poison to dip darts in for easier hunting. The student returned here for the summer and began experimenting with known poisonous plants and animals, and found there is a plant that can be cooked into a poison. By dipping different lengths and sizes of darts, he got darts for different sized animals. Hunters have been making them ever since. Come inside."

Brielle climbed the ladder. On one wall was a series of cylinders, each held a group of darts, which were just thin straight sticks sharpened to a point.

"None of these are lethal dosages. Just enough to bring down jumpers and stuff. Once the meat is cooked the poison is harmless. It has to go into your blood, not your stomach acid. We toss the used dart into the fire we use when we cook the jumper."

"How fast does it take effect?"

"Within two seconds the prey will start twitching, blinking if they have eyelids. Then they are down."

"Grown men?"

"Yes, though if the villager is wearing snakeskin the darts won't penetrate."

"The guards will be wearing cloth."

Brielle thought for a while. "Listen, you need to get me back to the village. That's my father leading them. He is not going to hurt me." She lied. Probably he would. She was useless to him now.

"But Brielle—" Nancy tried to protest.

"I was just exaggerating before, Nancy. He won't really hurt me."

The teens got pipes and darts, and placed them in small cups hanging from a strap around their waists.

"So, if I had a dart, could I just poke it into someone? Would the poison work?"

"Yes. We have to be really careful when dipping the darts and loading the pipes. That's why we have these."

Lizardskin gloves. Brielle quickly redid her long hair into a braid, and concealed several darts in it. She pulled on the gloves.

"Yeah, there was that time Jeremy shot himself in the foot. He was barefooted." T

The kids snickered. "It was a dose for a jumper so just made him dizzy."

"So if you shot, say, three darts into a man he would get more than dizzy?"

"Yes. He'd be temporarily paralyzed," Nancy said. "And if he had a heart condition or other health issues he could have a heart attack or a stroke, or breathing issues."

They arrived at the village and peered through the trees. The villagers were seated on the ground in the common area, with three armed guards surrounding them.

Silently the boys and Nancy determined which guard each one would shoot, and they brought up their pipes.

Brielle pulled several darts out of her hair and held two concealed in each hand. "Don't shoot," Brielle called as she stepped into the clearing. "It's Brielle."

Her father strode forward. "In the ship."

He grabbed her by the arm and one of the armed men moved forward to take her other arm. Brielle was terrified the other guards would fire on the villagers before the darts could stop them.

With a quick swing of her arms, she shoved darts into her father and his helper, hitting them in the thighs. They stumbled, fell, taking her down with them, but she scrambled away from them and turned to the villagers.

Their guards hit the ground. Villagers leaped up and took their weapons. The group of teen boys and Nancy stepped out of the woods, big grins on their faces. Brielle thought her heart might pound its way through her chest and slumped on the ground, limp. Two men rushed forward and took the weapons off her father and his man.

A half hour later Brielle was resting in her bed. Nancy brought her a meal and then a breathing treatment.

"After this, you need to rest. A gentle walk to the beach would have been fine, but traipsing about the jungle with those wild boys and poison darts!" The older healer waggled her head but smiled as she spoke.

She picked up the remaining dart Brielle had concealed in her hair. "I'm taking this down to the cook fire and getting rid of it. You take a nap."

"Yes, ma'am."

WHEN BRIELLE WOKE LATE that night Nancy was full of news. "Karvar and the men flying down to the Recondin station had been notified and were on their way back."

"Kyler had the military repositioned a satellite."

Brielle was so relieved communication had been restored. They would travel through the night and were expected by midday tomorrow. With any luck, she would sleep a good long while and when she woke it would nearly be time for Karvar to return. She could hardly wait.

Even if their marriage was going to end, he would be back with her, and safe. And for some reason she did not feel as pessimistic for their future as she had just a few days ago, maybe because she felt well. Tired, but fine.

Relieved her father had been caught and stopped was a big part of it. Maybe later she would feel a little heartbroken about that, but for now she was just glad it was over, and none of the villagers were harmed.

Her father and his men were recovered from the poison, but were tied up and under guard.

KARVAR RECEIVED A TEXT message on his com. The message was thrilling and yet terrifying. It seemed the drone that had found them near the village had transmitted enough data to Brielle's father that he could track them, concentrating on the northwest coast. He'd attempted to take the village hostage with some paid thugs, ex-military, but had been stopped by a group of kids with poisonous darts and blow pipes. And somehow Brielle had used darts on her father and a guard. Karvar could hardly wait to see her, to make sure she was all right. And find out how she came by poison darts.

The rescue party immediately turned their homemade aircrafts around and headed back to Culver Bay. He never should have left her, but it seemed like the logical thing to do to get Kyler's kids to safety and send a message to Kyler. Get this mess over with.

Kyler's kids were safe in the village.

I should have listened to my gut. While he tried to convince himself he was doing the smart thing, part of him inside was screaming, "Don't leave her!"

He wouldn't next time. Not unless she didn't want him around. His stomach tightened at that thought. But she seemed to like him. The sex was great for both of them, and she seemed to enjoy his company. He wouldn't know for sure until they were together again.

The propeller crafts arrived at the village around lunch time the next day. There were three Protectorate Fliers parked on the beach, two were big and lethal, those belonged to Kyler. The third was more utilitarian, a simple transport.

The Zh Cle' landed their small propeller crafts near the village and they all walked down a narrow path to the city center. Karvar jogged ahead, wanting to see Brielle, to make sure she was fine. He broke through the trees into the clearing and came to a stop.

His entire family that was still on New Prague was sitting at the communal tables. Father was having an animated conversation with a bunch of teenaged boys. Dessa, Tressa and Ambli were chatting with some village girls, who all sent covert glances toward Chip and Ty. Shay wasn't around.

Brielle turned and their eyes met. She stood and started toward him. He ran to her at full speed, picking her up and swinging her in a circle. Then he stopped and she pulled his face to hers for a kiss he would never forget. It was a kiss that told him they belonged together, forever.

When they came up for air he drew her a little out of the way, since the entire village was watching them.

"So sorry I left. What an idiot I was. All I could think about was getting back to you."

"I missed you but understood why you thought it was a good idea."

"Remind me next time I have some good idea that separates us that it will make me miserable."

She looked down. "I was pretty miserable, too."

He pulled her tight. "There is no reason at all we have to part. We're married... and I love you." He lost some breath as he spoke the last part.

Brielle threw her arms tight around his neck and looked right into his eyes. "I love you too, Karvar. And staying together makes me so happy and relieved. I want to be with you."

He grinned like an idiot for a minute until she kissed him, a kiss full of warmth and promise.

"How do you feel about your father?"

She shrugged. "I never really trusted him. Not like other children trust their fathers. Somewhere deep inside I think I always knew. The drugger wanted to control me, and my father wanted to control me."

Kyler wiped away a few tears.

After a while, then headed back to the village center. People were placing dishes of food on the table and the entire atmosphere was festive.

"So, tell me about these darts."

Her eyes got huge. "They work really fast! I poked my father and the guard with them in their thighs and boom! They were down."

"Amazing."

"And guess what else? Guess where the poison comes from?"

"A poisonous lizard."

She grinned. "No. Remember the neon orchid we went to see the night the station was firebombed? The poison is made from the petals."

He laughed as they joined the feast.

Epilogue

STAR GODS ABOVE, TY loved this place. Kyler had insisted the entire family stay in the Zh Cle' village for five days, learning of their concerns and just relaxing out of the public eye. Ty had gone fishing, done some surfing, learned how to fly one of those propeller crafts. It had been the best vacation ever.

He was leaving this morning for his tour of duty, but he knew he'd be back to this beach as soon as he had leave.

Ambli joined him on the beach. She slid off her shoes and stepped ankle deep into the water. They would be leaving for the domed city in an hour. He'd be taking a transport off New Prague in about twelve hours. The family was gathered, most of them sitting at the tables in the village where a festive breakfast had been presented.

"It was good seeing you again, Ty. I wonder when the whole family will be together again?"

He looked out toward the sea. "That's hard to say. I don't know where I'll be getting leave yet. I know I'll get leave time, but don't know if I can hitch a ride to New Prague."

"Your tour is three years?"

"Yes. Same as your degree. I'll have a long leave then. I think I might buy one of those premade house domes and set it up down here. Do some fishing, surfing..."

"I think there will be another wedding, maybe before then."

He frowned. "Not Dessa and Shay!"

"Of course not! When she found out Shay lied and was the daughter of one Commander Soule's mercenaries and not a factory worker, she dumped her like a hot rock. Got Tressa to help her drag Shay to Kyler to be arrested. Too bad you missed it, it was pretty funny."

Shay was back in the domed city, being questioned about her knowledge of the actions against Karvar and Brielle and if she spied on the family through her relationship with Dessa.

"I was talking about Grania and Chip."

Grania and Chip had joined them with almost no protest. They had found out they could work all morning on their projects and spend the afternoons at the beach.

Ty grinned. "I knew it, but didn't want to say anything until they talked to Kyler and Skyleen."

Kyler, who stood nearby watching the waves, grimaced. "Well, I was clueless, but Skyleen said she knew from back when they were twelve years old or so. This love stuff is all too complicated for me. Except for Skyleen, of course. She just made sense."

Ambli laughed

"Time to get settled, Ty." Kyler said. Ty was taking a transport to the military base, not the palace like the others. Ty gave hugs all around.

"Keep in touch, Ty." Ambli said.

He looked at her with her long hair shining in the sun. Did Ambli just make sense?

Well, not now. Maybe someday.

He hugged her. "I will, even though I might be moving around quite a bit."

"Me, too."

"What? You won't be at school on Terra?"

Her smile was mischievous. "I have a plan. Will catch you up when it is more defined."

"Right." He wanted to know more, but their lives were going in opposite directions. The family would keep an eye on her.

"So, Chen Chen it is?" Karvar asked Brielle as they waited to board their transport to New Prague Dome. Their plan was to a have her thoroughly checked out at the palace hospital, then take off on a real honeymoon. One with restaurants and soft beds.

She looked thoughtful. "What if we go to Farradae instead? Would that be all right?"

"Anxious to see your little sisters?"

She nodded. "I feel like I need to try and explain father's imprisonment to them, before they hear about it from others. I'm sure they will be fine living with us. Father spent little time with them anyway."

"I'm looking forward to it, always thought they were going to be a big part of our lives, because you spent so much time with them. Mom is all ready rearranging the palace for a family of four. She can do that while we are honeymooning on the white sands of Farradae."

Brielle kissed him

"It is a relief, knowing I will be their caretaker. I always had fears father would split them up for school, or send them off to school far away. Now I know I can keep them home with me. And you."

Karvar laughed. "We came to parenting pretty suddenly." He pressed a soft kiss on her forehead. "I do think everything will work out for us now."

Brielle was sure of it.

The End

About The Author

BIO

Take a bookworm. Hand her a stack of her much older brother's Sci-fi and fantasy novels, thrillers and horror comics. Then introduce the world of romance.

Make her a jinx. Every great genre TV show she loves gets the ax! So often the romances have no happy ending. She gets upset about no romance in the world and writes her own stories with happy endings.

Throw this all together, shake constantly, and pour onto a computer keyboard.

There!

You have me,

Melisse Aires

Find me!

I HAVE A NEWSLETTER! sendfox.com/melisseaires[1]

I can always be found on Facebook. I run the fun Scifi Romance Group[2] and also Romancing the Shire[3]. My personal group is Melisse Aires' Lair[4]

BLOG: https://melisseaireswriter.wordpress.com/

Website: http://www.melisseairesbooks.weebly.com[5]

Facebook: https://www.facebook.com/melisseaires

IO News Group:https://groups.io/g/MelisseAiresPureEscapism

Please review if you enjoyed this romance!

---

1. http://sendfox.com/melisseaires

2.   https://www.facebook.com/groups/the.scifi.romance.group/

3.   https://www.facebook.com/groups/romancingtheshire/

4.   https://www.facebook.com/groups/1732565730395151

5.   http://www.melisseairesbooks.com

Don't miss out!

Visit the website below and you can sign up to receive emails whenever Melisse Aires publishes a new book. There's no charge and no obligation.

https://books2read.com/r/B-A-PTK-AHEE

BOOKS 2 READ

Connecting independent readers to independent writers.

Did you love *Escaping Poison*? Then you should read *Pardblood, A Second Chance Romance*[6] by Melisse Aires!

A romance of second chances~

Dahr, Lord of the ancient and wealthy family Lhirandal, once rulers of planet Lumina, is dying too soon. He was poisoned a decade ago and has few days left.

His once strong family is in tatters.

Then Dahr has a vision. Or was it a visit from a long-gone ancestor?

Welcome the outcasts back to the family. The Pardbloods, with their feline characteristics, will give the family a future. The ancestor shows him a secret lab, and an ancient nano-formula that will save him.

It turns out to be real.

He must save the family.

---

6. https://books2read.com/u/baBaMv

7. https://books2read.com/u/baBaMv

Prenna's life goes by in a confusing blur. She struggles to raise her son and nephew, and appease her angry husband. She knows she is failing them all. Then one night a strange mist reclaims her mind, and her hidden Pard characteristics appear, as do the boys'. But her husband dies in the same mist.

She learns her nephew is the Heir to the most powerful family on Lumina. Soon Dahr brings Prenna and her children into his world of luxury, power, and high technology as he rebuilds his family.

Also by Melisse Aires

Another Supernatural Apocalypse
Enchanted Bonds
Ritual of Fire and Ice

A Warm Winter Fantasy
Elf Wish
Christmas Wizardry
Faunication

Cyborg Nation
A Cyborg's Old Terran Christmas

Diaspora Worlds
Her Cyborg Awakes
Alien Blood
Starwoman's Sanctuary
Escaping Poison
Cyborg Security

Diaspora Worlds Bundle
Cyborg Liberation

Encanto Bay--Where Magic Happens
White Tiger Lover
The Psyvamp and the Professor
Holly Jolly Vampire
Single Mom, Vampire Lover

Far Stars Universe
Stranded on Grzbt
Christmas Cookies in Space
Pardblood, A Second Chance Romance

Love on the Space Frontier
Stars Between Us

Realms of Glister
Orc In Winter
Bridal Faire

Urloon
Refugees on Urloon

Standalone
Her Accidental Angel
Warm Winter Fantasies Collection

www.ingramcontent.com/pod-product-compliance
Lightning Source LLC
Chambersburg PA
CBHW020718160726
47993CB00006B/2252